MY ALIEN
SPY

ROTHA MATES OF XAVIA | BOOK THREE

REVERIE HARWOOD

MY ALIEN SPY

Rotha mates of Xavia | Book Three

Reverie Harwood

This is a work of fiction. Names, characters, businesses, places, events, and incidents are either the products of the author's imagination or used in a fictitious manner. Any resemblance to actual persons, living or dead, or actual events is purely coincidental.

Cover design by Mayhem Cover Creations
Editing by Headlight Fluid Press

When they found a better planet,
Only the gentle survived
– Taylor Swift

Chapter One
Arriving in Colorado

Cassie

"Cassiopeia? That's an unusual name. Isn't that a star?" My ride-share driver peered from beneath thick eyebrows through the rear-view mirror.

I looked like a wet dog in the mirror reflecting back at him. My blond hair darkened with water, clinging to my face and making my big blue eyes look even larger and puppy like. Hopefully the tiredness masked the fear.

"A constellation, but I go by Cassie." I didn't feel like talking. It had been a long day before the time change, and I still wasn't to my destination.

The Peterson Space Force Base was near Cheyenne Mountain. Supposedly my family had been visited this base for an award ceremony, but I didn't recognize the airport. We probably wouldn't have flown commercial anyway. The car that picked me up today was new, pristine, and probably a rental. The driver was young, clean-shaven, and probably a soldier. I focused on keeping my sogginess contained.

"Your parents must really like astronomy," he said. "Are you one of those Space Girls?"

I didn't know what he was talking about. Just that some women could be astronauts? I was clearly not a soldier. Or maybe a 'space girl' was like a 'horse girl?' Whatever it was, it wasn't me. I shook my head and, mercifully, he stopped asking questions.

I rested my forehead on the car's window and watched the raindrops race across its surface like I did when I was a kid. I typically didn't get this intimate with the surfaces of a ride-share vehicle, but this one seemed clean enough. I fell asleep as soon as we got on the highway. I was tired.

Running away will do that to you.

"Ma'am," he said. Not because I was old enough to be a 'ma'am' but because he was trying to wake me up. "Can I drop you off before we get to the gate?"

"Yeah, that's fine." I waved with my hand before wiping the drool from my face. Maybe this base didn't like ride-share. I gathered my things, unplugging my phone from his console. Twenty percent battery—not bad.

He stopped the vehicle and jumped out to get my bags from the trunk. I stepped onto the sidewalk to get my bearings. We were a hundred yards from the gated entrance. Maybe I shouldn't have let him pick, but when he reappeared with my bags, I noticed his military haircut and the proper posture. I remembered it was a rental. Maybe this was his military base and he was moonlighting. I didn't want to get him in trouble. He probably needed the money.

Besides, I felt refreshed in the cool air after my nap. It had stopped raining, and my bag had wheels. It would be fine. I gave him a knowing smile as he left me on the road.

I felt less fine when he drove the hundred yards to the gate, deciding to go home for the night. Jerk.

Oh well.

I rolled up to the gate on foot and handed them my military ID. "I'm visiting my dad. Captain Smith."

They disappeared with my ID into the booth to make a phone call. I always imagined this part going south. That my dad would give the word and they'd cut up my ID and send me away, never to receive military discount benefits again.

While I had bet my last few hundred dollars on a one-way commercial flight here, my bet had been a good one. The private gave me my ID back.

"Where's my dad's place?" I asked, expecting to have to hoof it across half the military base.

Instead, the privates loaded up a golf cart with my luggage—a suitcase and a backpack—all of my worldly possessions. And I was driven, or maybe escorted, to the on-base housing. I took a deep breath of Colorado air. I had actually done it. I had run away. If Colin tracked my ride share, he would surmise my father was at Peterson, but he wouldn't be able to enter the base. I would have to be careful in the city of Colorado Springs, but hopefully Colin would give up after seeing I'd run to my dad. I didn't think he would be so daring, but I wouldn't make it easy for him either.

Most officers had nicer places off-base, but my dad for some reason liked the small, compact housing on the base or the military housing located near the base. He probably thought he was doing Space Force a favor by taking less. Maybe he thought that if we all cut back and trimmed the fat, we'd be an even greater and more powerful military force.

Whatever.

It made it easy for me to find him, and for Colin to not.

Despite having never lived on this base, its neighborhood appeared familiar. Probably because all military housing outfits were the same rectangles of hardy-plank ticky-tacky. However, the backdrop of the Colorado mountains in their glorious sunset colors were a big plus for this one. It still didn't distract me from my feelings of failure. I was admitting defeat.

*And the people in the houses all went
into the…military*

*Where they were put in boxes and
they came out all the same.*

I had tried to escape. I spent most of my years away in boarding school because my dad, as a single father, didn't know what to do with me. My mom named me Cassiopeia, and she potty trained me, and that's about where her and my story ended. I didn't blame her. I left as soon as I could too—at 17, freshly graduated from high school. I didn't belong in this ticky-tacky either. Even if it was the last place I wanted to be, at least I knew where my father was. And that he would help.

The private stopped at a house and double checked the number. There was no way to determine it was his other than that. The garage was empty, and I wouldn't necessarily recognize the car anyway. The house was the same as all the other houses next to it and all the other houses he'd lived in and I'd stay in during breaks.

The private unloaded my bags, and I waved him on with a thank-you. I didn't want him to realize I didn't have a key and have awkwardness ensue. I was already planning on waiting.

I walked to the stoop and waited, sitting on my gray flannel jacket. I checked the time. It was nearing five o'clock here. Unless he left work early to check on me, Colin wouldn't know I was missing for another two hours. My body tensed at the onslaught of text messages and phone calls I'd receive at that point. That time would come, but for now I'd enjoy the scenery. Past the square roofed houses was a beautiful pink and orange sky with mountains changing colors as often as the sun shifted. There were no mountains in Florida, and the sky had never looked so pretty when I was with Colin. He had quickly become my least favorite boyfriend, easily surpassing the boy in seventh grade who gave me a hickey with a vacuum to prove his sexuality, and the one who thought it would earn him brownie points with my dad if he dated me—he was trying to get into some space program. Actually, I don't know how that transaction played out. Whether it was the guy's idea or if my dad had handpicked him to be my spouse or whatever. Anyway, Colin. Worse than those two guys.

And, I was pretty sure I was pregnant.

That's why I had to get out. Because me getting pregnant was everything that Colin wanted, and, well, I wasn't sure. I had watched us grow more isolated. Things were going south and I was falling into this hole. He saw a baby as something that would bind us as a family. While having a family was everything I wanted too, I was pretty sure it was more about isolation and control for him.

So here I was at another man's doorstep. My dad's.

Trust me, I'd be somewhere else if I could. But I've allowed Colin to put so much distance between me and my friends, and, honestly, I didn't think they'd believe me. They loved Colin. They tolerated me. I couldn't trust that I wouldn't be dumped on his doorstep for us to work it out. They didn't know what we've done to each other. I doubted they'd believe or understand.

Chapter Two
My Father the Captain

Cassie

At exactly 5:15, a black Mazda pulled into the opening garage door with perfect right turn precision. Without the aid of a tennis ball hanging from the ceiling, my father parked perfectly within the bounds of the garage and closed the door without any backing up or correction. Just like the tight military corners of his bed sheets I could count on without even coming inside yet. I waited at the front door. I could hear him inside and could match all the noises with the routine of his life. Keys on the hook. Front porch light on.

He opened the door as the first moth fluttered to the light.

"Life harder than you thought, huh?" he said, turning his back to me as he cleared the foyer to the kitchen.

I followed him in like a puppy with its tail tucked between its legs. I don't think Captain Smith had ever felt like that, and even if he did, his straight-backed posture, strong shoulders, would never reveal it. I bee-lined to the refrigerator. I opened the fridge and saw the same twelve things. One of them being a case of Michelob Ultra. I opened one and handed it to him. He drank exactly one in the evening. I wasn't sure what the point of drinking so little of the swill was. He had probably read somewhere that the most successful people drink beer in moderation, and this was his interpretation.

Despite its meagerness, I figured he'd need the entirety of the bottle to deal with me. His oldest and possibly only trouble. He was doing great professionally as far as I could tell. Highly decorated. Genuinely modest. He was someone the military probably needed. But not me, well, damn, except in this moment. I needed him now.

"You may have one if you like," he said. It had been a big argument in our house many years ago. Even my rebellion felt painfully ticky-tacky.

I didn't have to feign my disgust. "Ew, no."

"I need a place to lay low for a while. Get back on my feet."

My dad chuckled over his beer. "I'm sorry, kiddo. I'm being deployed. They're going to put all my stuff in storage."

I looked past the kitchen and into the living room and now recognized the half-filled boxes in the room. Of course, he could have been moving in. I wondered how long he had even been here. Always moving. Maybe he was always in a state of a half-boxes now that I was gone. And here I was, back, and he was taking off.

"Where are you going?" Perhaps I could stay with him there. Suddenly the crappy plan I absolutely detested wasn't even a possibility. I was homeless.

My dad chuckled again, like I was the butt of a joke I didn't understand. I hated feeling as if I was losing a game. I couldn't stand it. Pride. Competition.

I searched my brain for something beyond the haze of the relation-shit that was Colin. What was in the news?

"Xavia? The vacation lark?" I asked. My father was a serious Space Force guy, not a tour guide for social media influencers and whoever else was into that space tourism thing.

"That's the one."

My eyes narrowed. Had my father gotten demoted? His face did not betray any disappointment though. And I knew the disappointed face well. Xavia was basically a tropical vacation but impractically far away—like Fiji. Xavia was Interstellar Fiji. I guess if Captain Smith was needed by his government, then he would be there.

Wait. What the hell? Could I fucking go to Xavia? My eyes widened, and a rare smile crept on my dad's face.

"Any more room on that ship?" I tried to ask casually, but my demeanor had already broken. Even if it had to be in a shipping container like River in *Firefly*, I would be happy to get on that ship. Colin sure as hell couldn't follow me there. And it was a whole planet, right? Once we got there, I didn't have to be under my father's care. We could live on the same planet. We'd been doing it on this planet sort of OK.

"I'll see what I can do. There's a program for young women on the ship, traveling independent women— you'd fit in there."

"A program?" Somehow, I didn't think pregnancy would fit their eligibility requirements for a traveling independent woman. "I don't think I'll qualify."

"Christ, Cassie."

I swore that was my name, Christ Cassie.

"Which part?"

"Um, the bloodwork part."

My dad's brown eyes bored into me. When I was younger, I thought it was an interrogation technique he'd picked up in the military. At some point, my discomfort and guilt would tip over and I'd confess. As I got older, I could withstand longer, and now, I realized that was the only thing in my father's arsenal. He was silent because he didn't have the balls to ask the hard questions or to accuse me.

"OK. We might be able to get around that." He finally said, unable to inquire any further.

And that was the end of the emotionally tense, highly unsatisfying conversation. He pulled sheets from a box marked *BEDDING* and made up the couch with precise tucks. Instead of saying good night, he said, "No drugs in my house." We're a loving family.

At least he was here for me. I couldn't say the same about my mom. My dad and I were two strangers tied together by a woman who had left us both. She discarded his name after giving me mine. I still wasn't sure how she got such an eccentric name past him. Maybe he felt guilty about tying her down. I always figured me and my name were some of the last efforts to keep them together.

I was torn about my own pregnancy. I cared enough about my unborn child to run away from Colin. However, did I want to give birth to it? If I did, I'd forever be bound to that man.

I no longer trusted him. Actually, I had stopped trusting him long before he hit me. I had considered my exits before, but now it was the eleventh hour and I needed somewhere to go. My baby and I needed somewhere to go.

I don't know if my dad abused my mom with anything more than dull monotony and olive drab. She traded me and him in for whimsy or some shit. And with my name, she'd left me a map for my exit.

Maybe I, Cassiopeia, would be heading to the stars.

Chapter Three
A Hoax

Zade

Complete darkness was always a comfortable feeling like a cool blanket. It was the sort of darkness in which one could get confused as to whether their eyes were open or closed. I sat on the tunnel's floor, my ankles digging into the smooth stone. I knew my eyes were closed because I was thinking too much. I was caught up in my own body and my senses. I should be focused on the mine, its acids and bases. Bern approached.

Who was I kidding? My father was much better at finding veins of glor, an ability our family called 'glor-minding.' He and his father had created a vast network of mines before the Orkain interrupted our civilization. Prince Drex gave away what glor we had and tasked me with matching my father's projections after his death.

All of my recent attempts had been in vain. Sitting in the dark emptiness, I wondered if it really was. I could be doing something wrong. My father had pierced the bridges of our noses, convinced it helped with glor-minding—metals reacting in our very bodies.

Had he been mistaken about his projections? Had he lied to our government?

Was glor-minding even a real thing?

If my father had been planning to give up his secrets, he didn't have the chance. He died several subsystems above this one. We hadn't met the humans yet. His mines were on the verge of being shut down. His accident seemed like a careless mistake, but I wondered if he just didn't want to adapt to our new lives after the Orkain killed his wife and nearly every other Xavian he'd known.

That was a depressing thought.

Invasive, like these mines.

I returned to my bones on the stone. Mimicking my father's stance, probably a younger mirror image of him before he spent his life in the mines looking for… what? Glor? Glory?

We shared silver-purple hair, like quartz against our turquoise skin, opalescent dark features, horns, and a functional strength. We didn't have the necessary broadness of soldiers or the vanity broadness of royalty. Those types couldn't fit into these mines where that strength would be needed. Still, weakness meant death down here. I was strong.

"Sir. I'm sorry to bother you," said Bern, unable to hide the excited lilt in his voice.

I made no movement from my meditative state. In his attempt to woo one of the remaining Xavian women, Bern had bulked up to what was more than practical. He snaked his shoulders through the narrow crevice to reach my pocket of space.

Bern may have thought this was enough space for two people, but it was not. His presence encroached on mine. I cracked an eye open, forced to acknowledge his presence.

"Uh, yes, sir. Vance is on the surface to see you."

As if this was not already an invasion. Now I had to interrupt all that I was doing, because Vance, adviser to the prince, happened to be walking on the surface and wanted to know what was going on. Worse, nothing was going on. I had made no progress. The projections of glor that my father presented to their fathers? As far as I can tell, that was a bunch of bullshit. However, we've sold that bullshit to the humans on Earth. They are willing to live here on Xavia and bolster our dying species through interspecies sex.

However, even with the demand for glor, there were Xavians who didn't think it should be a continued industry with our population loss. They'd rather those resources go elsewhere. Unfortunately, Vance was one of those people. He wanted to use the mining technology to create tunnels and homes for the surviving Xavians.

I did not think the solution was to hide away, and that was coming from someone who spent much time underground. Bern provided his hand and used his own weight to provide leverage to help me rise. The blood rushed into my legs as I shook them out.

"I'll take over for you," he joked as he released my hand.

Bern had no such gift, and I wondered if he believed the skill existed. I wasn't sure if I did at this point. Our people weren't religious. Spiritual, yes. Religious or organized? No, and we believed our science would soon catch up with whatever it was that I or my father sensed in these caverns. It would be sure to be some scent or some electromagnetic wave we had tuned into. I'd be explained by science then replaced, sure enough, by technology.

Hopefully soon, because I was a little lost.

Not in a physical sense though. In these mines, I wound in and out, up and down, until I'd reached the surface where Vance stood. He tapped his hands on his crossed arms in a sign of impatience. For someone who wanted us to live underground, it amused me he'd stayed up here. Was he afraid of getting lost? What about when he was in his precious tunnel system?

"Zroso," I said hiding my smirk. The address came from position, not from his personal history. Offices were usually held by elders with decades of experience. Our generation had been thrust into these positions without earning them. It would take another generation or two removed to know if they were doing any of the right things.

"You were selected," he said over my shoulder, not looking at me directly.

Of all the reasons Vance would come speak with me, this one I wasn't expecting. I was eligible as a single male, but I never thought for a moment they'd select me to court a human woman. What did I have for one except a cave and a job that took up all of my time? There were plenty of Xavians who actually wanted the opportunity. I'd have thought it a joke, but Vance wasn't finding any pleasure in telling me the news.

We were somewhat rivals. We had opposing opinions for what we thought was best for the Xavian people. I believed our best hope lay with the holmium in our veins. We gave it to Earth because they were our only hope of continuing our species. If we could breed with the humans, our race would not die out. And Vance argued that we needed to keep the people we currently had safe, and to him that meant that we should dig tunnels to hide from the Orkain that flew above our heads. If only things were that simple.

Things weren't that simple. Vance was a dummy with the prince's ear. And why? Because they were best friends growing up. What a fantastic way to run a branch of government. Of course, it probably wasn't much better to gain control over a Xavian resource through your father.

"Do you think they will come back?" I asked. We'd given the humans all of our glor supply, but they might never return with their end of the deal.

"Of course," he said with the tone of a politician, slick with the confidence their idiocy earned them. "Better get your place ready. Clean it up."

Why was I being given this "honor?" I hadn't helped give the humans glor so that I could personally benefit. I didn't want help finding a mate. I wanted to find more glor to replace what we'd lost from our system forever.

What a mess we had made.

Chapter Four
Military Treatment Facility

Thankfully, my dad didn't make me go in at the ass-crack of dawn with him. He had arrangements to make first. It gave me time to sleep, shower, and retch into the toilet. The morning sickness had started. It felt familiar, like a daily hangover for my horrible mistakes. Another reminder was Colin blowing up my phone. His voice-mails ranged from sweet pleads to screaming, calling me a slut, and accusing me of cheating on him. He said we weren't broken up because you can't do that in a note and that I needed to talk to him.

I was not going to do any such thing.

A few hours and one piece of toast later, there was a knock on the door.

A pimply enlistee announced he was here to escort me to the MTF, military treatment facility. He stumbled over his words, not anticipating a lone civilian. Maybe he thought a family member should be with me. Nope. I was used to being transported from base to base, one military personnel to another, as my father was always doing more important things. I was below the captain's pay grade and rank.

So instead, this young man drove me across the base much like he spoke, jerkily, which did nothing for my anxiety or nausea. He probably could have driven better if he'd stopped looking over at me. He maybe hadn't seen a live woman in civilian clothes and with long hair in months. Now he was inches from one in some sort of modified golf-cart, sanctioned to be faster than feet but not quite golf-cart speed.

Faster-than-feet was still too fast for my sour stomach. Thankfully, the cold air bit into my lungs and provided an appreciated distraction. Not soon enough, we pulled to the front of the MTF.

"Um, good luck," he said, looking straight ahead. It was like he was refusing to admit he was dropping me off to something significant.

"Thank you," I said. I moved onto the sidewalk and pretended to look for something in my purse as he drove off slowly.

When he turned the corner, I walked around the corner of the clinic and vomited into the bushes. Then I wretched twice more. Wiping the gunk from my chin, I spotted a bench on the side of the building, probably for the staff to come out and smoke.

I put a stick of spearmint gum in my mouth and chewed, a tummy remedy from my childhood since my father rarely allowed me to miss school. It would at least get the nasty taste out of my mouth. I tried not to focus on the acids rolling around on my tongue and in my stomach. In the distance, guardians marched in formation, a familiar rhythm and pattern. Order and cleanliness, ticky-tacky.

A tall woman with a big nose came around the corner. She had on white scrubs which contrasted with her sunbaked skin. Her white tube socks peeked out from large white sneakers.

"Are you Cassiopeia Smith?" she asked. She towered over me.

"I am," I said slowly, trying to think of an excuse for being out here, probably late for my appointment.

"I'm Tabitha."

Tabitha paused to give me a once-over, possibly to make a medical assessment and personal judgement. She didn't scold me or gesture for me to come inside. Instead, she sat down on the bench beside me.

"Captain Smith told me about your situation. It's all worked out. Just come inside. We'll get you on the ship."

For being my savior, she didn't sound too excited about it. She probably wasn't regularly asked to send an unqualified woman into space. What had he concocted to get me on the ship that didn't risk his squeaky-clean image?

"Lead the way," I said, curiosity overcoming my nausea. Would he learn about my pregnancy? I felt some relief in not having to tell him myself.

Tabitha's knees creaked as she returned to her full height. We managed to brush the conspiracy off our pants and turn professionalism on when we got inside. Tabitha took my vitals and my body measurements in some combination of a doctor's visit and a dress fitting. When it came to bloodwork, Tabitha fitted herself with a torniquet and drew her own blood into vials.

"During travel, your body will metabolize things more slowly, but it'll still be long enough to get you through the detox and any withdrawal symptoms," she explained.

I stared at her stupidly for a solid beat before I realized Tabitha and my dad thought I was taking drugs that were going to exclude me from the program. This was my dad's way of getting around it. Tabitha had probably never taken a drug in her life, and she thought she was helping my dad get his daughter into the weirdest drug rehabilitation program ever. I mean, I had heard of being "sent off," but this was wild. I guessed anything for the messed up captain's daughter, getting passed along for the ride. She must have assumed my nausea on the way in was from withdrawal. Damn.

My dad was an asshole for assuming I was on drugs (this time), but I didn't quite know what to do about it. Should I clear up this misunderstanding? Should I come clean about being, well, clean? No. I needed a place to live; I needed on this space ship. So, yeah, I probably needed this nurse's blood. My dad had everything worked out.

I didn't have time for the guilt to overcome my hesitation. Tabitha walked out with the vials in a bag marked with my name, and that was that. It only became more awkward after that, because she then brought in several suits for me to try on, explaining that they were back-ups for the other women. Every single one was snug in one or more places. My big, curvy body didn't fit their social media influencer demographic. What did the ride-share driver call them? *Space Girls*. Embarrassingly, they gave me a suit that was a different color than the others, but it fit much better.

"You'll be wearing that one tomorrow," she said, shaking her head. I wasn't sure if it was in disbelief that I didn't fit into those tiny suits or that I was going into freaking space tomorrow.

I took a deep breath. I hoped we survived the trip. And if not, I wouldn't have to tell my dad about my pregnancy mess-up. What a crazy thing.

Chapter Five
Preparations

Zade

The skies were dark outside when I reached the mine's entrance—my exit. I was late again. I leaned against the interior wall, solid and sturdy, letting my eyes adjust. I'd lost track of time. It was safer to sleep here than to venture into the cool darkness where my body's heat could be detected by the Orkain. However, if my human guest arrived, I'd be expected to return home each evening. Another reason to return home—they were scheduled to land in the next few solars and I'd yet to finish preparations.

Seeing no Orkain in my time by the threshold, I dashed to the line of trees. Nothing screamed out or rushed me with wings. The possibility of being caught greatly diminished, my tired brain directed me home without much thought to anything else. My home was as close to the mine as my grandfather had been allowed to build it. My legs and eyelids dragged. This was my favorite way to go to bed, exhausted and unthinking. I liked to work until I could not, and then… all-encompassing sleep.

I stumbled into my home in my tiredness. I averted my eyes from the unfinished chores. It's not like I didn't know what needed to be done. I had grown up in this home doing these chores. I was supposed to come home when it was still daylight to complete the landscaping and to dust the place. I'd forgotten…again. Now, I was too tired. It would have to wait until morning.

In the dust room, I took off my boots and dirty clothes, stripping to my underwear. If Mom had been there, I would have showered, but as she wasn't, I shuffled across the floor to my thick bed, planting face-first into the pillow, and slept.

I awoke many hours later and rolled onto my back. My legs protested, the muscles heavy and the joints ungreased. My chest and face cheeks expanded slowly as if compressed for the entire night. Artificial light timers weren't available when my grandfather built his home into a cavern. I grew up without them, and as an adult, my work and sleep schedules were not subject to such things. However, like the Xavians who moved into homes modeled after mine upon arrival of the Orkain, a human guest may want such a device. I added it to my mental list of things to do.

I skipped cleaning my room; she wouldn't see it. I'd procrastinated many solars in the mines, rationalizing my home didn't need much work and that the women might not even arrive. Now, I surveyed the bathing room. I wasn't here often, nor did I often clean. The bathing room needed the most work by far, and I set to doing it. I settled into scrubbing it top to bottom. I wouldn't want her to be grossed out. She was alien. She might already be grossed out by me. Her species' men were much softer than us. It showed how rich they were. We did not have that luxury. Our bodies were hard. We needed our strength to contribute to society and to keep safe. Here in Xavia, we had to run and fight.

I used my strength to scrub around the shower fixtures that utilized the cave's spring and thus were built up with minerals. My nasal passages began to burn with the chemicals I'd borrowed from the mines to cut down on my cleaning time. I wiped the sweat from my upper lip and turned the ventilation on high. The fumes evacuated to disperse in the stiff breeze outside.

I turned to the less difficult work of the mirror, reaching for the top but then realizing the lights above it had dust. I sighed and started wiping the grimy dust from top to bottom that had settled on the light fixtures like a sludge. Gross. I pulled them down to soak the glass bulbs in the sink. Unable to finish the sink, I moved to the toilets.

I was going to be pissed if Drex made me clean my toilet for nothing. Although it did need to be done. I'd been in denial up until…well, now…but it made sense I'd be chosen to host. I was of the appropriate demographic and educated in the desired metal. The ones with more peers in their industry had more competition. Those had possible home visits and a prying eye for issues or supremacy. If anything, they should feel lucky as they'd all cleaned their toilet bowls more recently than I had.

Maybe it would be good to have someone else here to help keep the place clean. If the volunteers arrived, I got to bring one home. If they didn't arrive, then my glor-minding problems would be solved. I didn't mind going over the ring in the bowl one more time. It needed it anyway.

I stepped back and looked at my work. I had done pretty well. I only had…the rest of the house to clean. I groaned. I stopped myself from touching my itchy nose piercing with a dirty hand. This woman had better show up. I had better things to do.

Chapter Six
Mission

Cassie

My eyelids felt like heavy gates as I eased them open to their first light in…months? I tried to shake my head. My muscles responded as if they were coated in molasses. Slowly coming out of it, I noticed restraints. My eyes fluttered open then. I was in a stasis pod and had been for quite some time. I had been put to sleep, and now I was waking. I worried I was waking at the wrong time. That movie crossed my mind. IVs and tubes came from my body. I was secured at my wrists and couldn't tilt my head down.

The clear acrylic in front of me became opaque, and I think I screamed. No sound came out. Or if it did, it didn't reach my ears. Would anyone else hear me with their own sleep-addled ears? Before I could panic about not being able to move, and now see, a video was projected on the white acrylic, my own personal screen. It was my father in his military garb, behind a desk—an official video—but it was also only for me.

"Cassiopeia. You were placed with a group of women who are being delivered to the Xavians for a year-long genetic exchange." He paused, but not long enough for me to be able to understand or swallow the meaning of a genetic exchange. And, delivered? He wasn't staying.

"The Xavian species is critically endangered, and they have knowledge about their extensive holmium mines—a rare Earth metal they call glor. Over this year, please gather as much information as you can on glor—how much they have, how it is mined, and the major players involved." What was this, a mission? I wasn't his soldier. This wasn't my job. I pulled against my wrist restraints and ground my teeth, seething in anger, I remained silent and begrudgingly alert. I might only get to hear this message once.

A photo of a blue-green humanoid with purple hair was presented on the screen. He had a human nose, mouth, lips. He also had swirling starry eyes and horns that sprouted on his forehead and curled over his eyes like eyebrows. He had a piercing through the bridge of his nose. Damn, he was hot. Did all the aliens look like this?

"This is Zade. He is in charge of the mines. Get to know him."

Even his name was sexy… Zade.

"America needs this information to make sure they're getting a fair deal."

Harrumph, I laughed. More like to milk Xavia dry. I didn't fall for that patriotic bullshit. My dad hadn't said outright whether I'd be taken back to Earth if I gave him this information. While I wanted to ignore everything my father said, I wasn't stupid. I paid attention to what he considered valuable. If I chose to gather the information, I would not blindly turn it over. I'd use it to negotiate my seat on the next flight home.

And we were here for a year for a genetic exchange? What the fuck? Save the Xavians by having sex with them?

I'd heard of some bonkers government plans, but this had to be a joke. I couldn't imagine my government trafficking women. What slimeballs. And what did that make my dad? He sent his own daughter here. Scummier than scum.

It turns out there was plenty of time to be angry and then panicked and then to listen intently again, because the stupid video played ten times before the straps released. By then, I heard others moving in their rooms. I didn't know if they'd seen a different video or knew anything at all. I felt sick with my small amount of information. And scared.

I gently released myself from my crypt, deflating this, pulling out that, removing the IV. I knew what to do based on the tools provided to me. I clipped my nails. My clearest thought was that I wasn't nauseous. I'd experienced morning sickness, and while this wasn't necessarily morning, it felt like a waking, and yet I didn't feel ill. What did that mean? Was I still pregnant? Maybe they discovered my pregnancy and terminated it. I needed more information before I panicked. I put the disturbing thoughts aside so that I could venture into the hallway.

When my dad said I'd fit the demographic, I didn't know he meant lost and confused women in their twenties. They talked about haircuts while I checked the doors. We were trapped in here with no access to food stores. If we were being dropped off, we were being dropped off with nothing. We would be reliant on the Xavians.

Hopefully our interactions went well. A few others began checking doors and voicing concerns about not seeing any staff.

"Has anyone seen room service?" one girl asked.

The televisions clicked on in all the rooms simultaneously. My father appeared on everyone's screen, including mine. The sound came from the pods.

"Thank you for participating in our cultural exchange mission. We have been clear on the importance of this program, but not *how* it is important. You see, you have been chosen to save this planet in a genetic exchange. This planet has two important resources. One is holmium, known to us as a rare Earth metal. It's critical in all of our industries, space-travel, surface-travel, medical, communication, computers, defense. The second resource is the natives that maintain the mines. You are here for the second, their species is on the edge of collapse. They are lacking females, and your wombs are the only things that can save this species."

"Oh shit," the women said in chorus. And a lot of cursing at my father. He deserved it. My special video had given me information, but it did not comfort me. He seemed to think I'd survive spending time with the Xavians, but I wasn't so sure. What were we in for?

We didn't have much time to dread the idea. I couldn't tell that we were moving, but everyone knew when we stopped. Our bodies were jarred. Many who were standing had fallen to the ground. We had reached out destination.

Chapter Seven
Stupidity

Zade

I groaned, checking the time. No. I was not late. In fact, I had a few moments to enjoy the quiet. Although I wasn't convinced, there was a chance, that I could have a guest today. I would believe it when I saw it. Just in case, I'd finished cleaning.

I remember complaining as a child that the walls were stone, dusty, and thus there was no point to cleaning the dust. Now I knew the erosion slowly made our home larger…very slowly. Maybe my mom thought she could speed along the process. She would have me dusting and taking the dirt out of the cave every day. Now I did the same, in case it was more than only my eyes seeing these walls and living within them.

I soaked in the tub, not because I needed to, but because it helped me connect to the world in the mornings. Not just sleeping on comfy things inside the cave, but soaking in its waters held up by its walls. The solidness of the place, built from a cavern digging thoughtfully into the cliff-face, had made a beautiful location for its time. One day, maybe thousands, maybe hundreds of thousands of years from now, it would be gone. What would I have done within its walls?

Nothing yet.

That's why I couldn't decline this opportunity to pair with…well, anyone. My job had left no time to date or spend time with anyone left in our dwindling community. If I was to leave a legacy in glor, I would need to pass on my knowledge to somebody in the next generation. It didn't necessarily need to be my own bloodline. The knowledge was important enough to pass on. We already had industries lost. There was texts and manuals, but the people who made it run— gone. Losing knowledge of how to find and extract glor would set the Xavian people back and increase their reliance on foreign markets, like Earth.

We had to be protective of our remaining population, which was why I nearly left in protest when I saw how many people had gathered for the arrival of the ship. What was the prince thinking? I understood the hosts coming to pick up their guests. I was one of them. I understood the argument for having Xavian women to soften a potentially scary situation, but it was risky. They could have counseled through virtual channels.   And the onlookers? Absolutely not. If I was a prince, I would order them home immediately.

Drex did not. Instead, he and Vance looked upon us with excitement. I tried to keep Drex and Vance within eyesight. I hated not knowing what was going on. Instead, I stood with the rest of the idiots in a couple of too-large groups. The men spoke loudly and punched each other's arms and shoulders. I was surprised the dummies weren't locking horns. Oh, no, those two were. In a game to encourage each other, they burned off nervous energy.

Drex was correct about the arrival. A fireball made its slow descent and landed a short distance from us. We moved en masse without needing Drex's gestures and shouts. Did he think us dumb? Probably. I was amazed he'd managed such a negotiation, but I guess we'd see what came out of the ship.

We approached the clearing and saw the 'ship' was much smaller than the first one that had negotiated the deal. It was the same wet stone gray as the first, but had nothing of its engines either. It seemed to have been dropped off of a bigger ship. The long metallic capsule had a ramp and a door that opened to our newest mystery.

Drex sent in the group of women without any guards. His incompetence pissed me off. If the Xavian women were supposed to expedite the process, they didn't, as only Lowree came out to speak with Drex. Like the other men, I grew impatient. It was possible the Orkain had seen the pod, or even the ship before it, and were on their way to investigate. We needed to clear this place out. Did Drex not have an exit plan for us?

Chapter Eight
Alien Greeting

Cassie

I walked down the hallway, seeing other women getting to their feet in their rooms. A previously locked double door was wide open with light pouring in, and the pod suddenly felt exposed. A ramp of the gray metal reached down to a green planet. I crept along the wall, curious to see Xavia but fearful of what I might find.

It was wild.

Did we land in a jungle, or just how populated was this planet? Oh, right. Not heavily populated and in need of women. Something thick and heavy sank in my chest, filling me with dread.

"Hello!" called out someone in English. "You've arrived on Xavia. Welcome! Is everyone OK?"

I jumped back as I saw green people...Xavians...emerge from the jungle. *Not me* was the only thought in my mind. I wasn't a leader. I would not be the one to speak out.

"We're OK!" shouted someone behind me.

That seemed like a stupid thing to shout. How did she know? Had she talked to everyone on the ship after their tumble? And also, I felt our "okayness" was highly dependent on who was outside. Whatever, being led "wrong" was the consequence of not-leading. I stayed back.

Yellow-green aliens plodded up the ramp and peeked through the door.

The brunette that shouted bravely approached them. "I'm Katy. You speak English?"

"Yes, we're so excited for your arrival. We've all tried to learn your language so that you'd be more comfortable. The men sent us so that maybe you'd feel more comfortable." She repeated the word.

"So you are women? There are women here?" Katy asked.

"Yes, we're female." The woman gestured and four other women came in. Two of them had extra rounded bellies and I wondered if they were pregnant. "I'm Lowree. We are some of the few females left."

I didn't expect to feel sorry for the Xavians, but at least these women seemed innocent with their friendly welcome. But the casualness as to why we were here?

Another woman spoke up. "Look, I'm not sure what you thought was going on, but we just got baited and switched here." The woman's dark features flashed angrily.

"Baited and switched?" asked Lowree, hesitantly. Of course she didn't understand the term.

Katy explained to Lowree (and to me). "Our government told us that both men and women were coming on this journey to visit, and we would experience your culture. But then, we just saw a message from our government. They say they made a deal with you to, um…copulate? Do you know that word?"

Lowree said she did. "They…baited and switched…lied to you. They were dishonest?" She was catching on.

"Fryyre," she muttered. I didn't have to know the language to understand that it was a curse word. "Let me talk to the prince. You all can come if you like, but maybe it's best if everyone's intentions are made clear before they see you all. You all are…beautiful."

Lowree hiked down the ramp to the men of their species, who were taller, bluer, and with horns. That was as long as I could stand to watch as I was being stared at by the Xavians who had gathered. The population ratio was blatant, and I was supposed to be a womb for them. How many of them? Mine was already occupied, I hoped. I dropped my hand away from my belly as if it would give away my condition.

Lowree's face was ash gray as she raced forward with several Xavian men behind her.

"We have to go now. The Orkain are coming."

"The Orkain are here," said a male behind her.

I did not know who the Orkain were. Exchanging glances with the other women convinced me they did not know either. I wasn't supposed to know… Something our government and my father hadn't shared.

Katy began organizing the women behind me, sending someone to pull everyone into the hall. The Xavian women were already being escorted off the ship. Their welcome seemed short-stayed, but if there were valuably few women, I guessed they needed protection. That's all the convincing I needed to exit the ship.

Like a storm was brewing, the green trees swayed and clouds swirled. I looked into the jungle and couldn't locate the source of the effect. Xavians were scattering, disappearing into the thickness of the jungle, but they stole glances behind them to the ship and above us. That's when I realized the danger wasn't going to come from the depth of the jungle but from the skies. What would be big enough to cause these Amazonian-like people to scatter? What had decimated these people?

A winged beast with devilish horns and tail flew across the clear sky above the ship. The creature was red—not like the color of cartoons—but a deep, blackened hue. A massive arm surrounded me and pulled me over the ramp's side. I fell into shrubbery and onto the owner of the massive arm.

"Zade." It slipped from my mouth, in a daze as his beautiful face filled my view. It wasn't a photo anymore. His silver purple hair flowed, speckled eyes spun, and a large bar disappeared from one side of his nose and reappeared on the other side with a chain connecting the outside ends.

His eyes widened and spun even faster at the sound of his name. Oh shit. I'm pretty sure we weren't supposed to know their names.

"Heyy, D" I tried to make his name sound like a greeting as I clambered off of him. It was an awful attempt. I grimaced and hoped he wouldn't remember in the chaos. His broad hand was wrapped around my forearm, urging me to follow him. Beside me, a woman was being helped forward by an even larger broad-shouldered man. He looked like a green boulder pushing along a blond damsel.

We ran from the small pod even as more filed out. I soon lost sight of it as we moved into the quieter parts of the jungle. Now I could only hear our footsteps and the biggest of the Xavian men breaking branches ahead.

Chapter Nine
Escaping

Zade

How did this beautiful creature know my name?

She had the palest skin I'd seen, with a thin set of tiny spots along her cheeks that held up beautiful blue eyes—no hint of the green or yellow of my species—pure blue circles around blackness that might be nothing at all.

She seemed just as surprised by my name coming from her lips. More incoherent words tumbled out as she hastily stood up. Adrenaline rushed through me. I was afraid of the Orkain, oddly distracted by her touch, and confused by the interaction. I jumped up beside her. I wanted to shield her, hold her, keep her from the Orkain. I settled with a hand on her arm, leading her into the jungle. Moto, one of the soldiers, barreled past us with a human in tow. She had deep reddish-brown hair hiding big, round, scared eyes. The humans were smaller and wore metallic suits—making them easy to spot. They were so much smaller and weaker than us. They needed protecting.

I drove the woman who knew my name deeper into the dense jungle, making sure we would disappear into safety. It was an escape route I'd planned even as we walked here. Everyone should have had one, but it was clear they had not. With bad leadership, people die.

I veered her away from where the jungle met the water. My first choice was a cavern ahead. Its mouth was defensible, and there were multiple routes through the caves. Despite having pushed past us earlier, Moto took a more circuitous route and ended up behind us.

I waited for them, expecting Moto to be unfamiliar with the cave system and the attached mines.

"Follow me."

No one followed. The two women huddled together away from both me and Moto. They looked warily at us. With the Orkain out of sight, we were the potential threat.

"No, I want to stay here," said the blond.

She remained frustratingly close to the mouth of the cave. If we could walk into this cave, so could the hunting Orkain.

"I can protect this entrance," Moto said, his stupid soldier persona shining. That didn't help. There was no point in defending this location when I could take her back to my home. I was losing control of the situation.

"My name is Layla," offered the woman who was with Moto.

"I'm Cassie."

"Wait, do you know my name?" I asked Layla. Here I would get my answers.

Layla's lips and eyelids crinkled. "No, I don't. I'm sorry. What is it?"

Layla didn't know my name, so why did the other one? *Cassie* knew my name. I turned to her. She was resolutely silent. Her small eyes bore into mine.

"I'm Zade. I cannot let you stay here. It's not safe. Please follow me."

Chapter Ten
A Place to Land

Cassie

I was the worst spy ever.

I didn't mean to say his name. It slipped out. What were the chances he'd be the one to tackle me, anyway? I appreciated him getting me to cover, but now I wanted to stay with the other woman, Layla. I didn't know her, but there was safety in numbers. And her escort was even larger than Zade.

"Layla, come with us," I said. We'd be safe together…probably.

"No, I am caring for Layla. I'm Moto," butted in Layla's rescuer.

"One guest per host," declared Zade.

Layla and I exchanged glances. It felt like a delicate situation. I didn't want to stay in this cave or leave Zade for Moto and Layla. Layla shook her head. She would stay with Moto.

All right.

"Can we help Layla and Moto get to where they're going then?" I asked. I didn't want her left here in the cave.

Zade hesitated—then, "Yes, we can do that."

Moto did not seem pleased by the arrangement, and Zade did not hide his smirk well. I tried to give him the benefit of the doubt, but he acted like he'd won an argument or contest. And that sort of pissed me off.

Zade walked fast. We covered a lot of ground, or…well, underneath it. The tunnels were tall, sometimes uncomfortably narrow, and had dips and rises for much longer legs than mine.

"What do you mean one guest per host?" I asked. Was that the lodging situation?

"Is there no hotel here?" asked Layla.

"Hotel?" asked Moto.

"A place with private rooms for rent. For temporary stays," I explained.

"No, we don't have that anymore. Stay with hosts in their homes. Communal is for men," said Zade.

"What did our government say about us? What do you think this is?" My dad lied to me, lied to Layla and the rest of these ladies… He had likely lied to these people too.

"You are volunteers to live on Xavia and cohabitate with us."

"First of all, we aren't. We were told… What were you told, Layla?" I asked.

"I was given a free vacation. It was supposed to be six months, but now they said they aren't coming back for one year…"

"And you?" Zade asked me.

"I was told the same thing. They tricked us. We didn't know your people needed women. Or what this place was like."

"They didn't tell you about the Orkain," said Zade.

"Fryyre," muttered Moto.

"That's what the lady said. So, we were sold to you," I guessed.

"We'd never buy women…" said Zade.

"What did you give them?" I asked. I already knew the answer.

"Glor."

As soon as he said it, I realized we were probably in its vicinity. The walls appeared to be packed dirt, the concrete and wood framework surrounded us. The corded lights strung above my head were glowing fibrous vines. Where did all these tunnels lead?

"Did your people create these tunnels?" I asked.

"My family did," he replied.

That was impressive. "For what? For glor?"

Zade grunted and walked faster.

"How do mine glor?" I hurried my pace to match his.

He didn't answer. I guessed he didn't want to talk about it. I had lost all perspective of where I might be. It was blowing my mind that I was underground on a planet that wasn't Earth.

Two more twists and, suddenly, sunshine, but not my sun.

"How far did we go?" I asked.

"Not as far as you would suspect," he said. "Moto and Layla will go that way. We will go this way."

Layla grabbed me in a hug that was clearly goodbye. She had made her decision. I guess it was the devil you knew, or in this case, the one you knew for a few minutes and now were making a gut decision about. I hoped I would see her again. I needed to stay with Zade.

His long arm corralled me as we walked through the jungle, but his eyes were on the sky.

"Are there more of the…what did you call them?" Something that sounded like orcs. They looked just as ugly, with horns that twisted into their face.

"Orkain. There are many, but they hunt solo. We will likely not encounter another."

I wondered if we'd encounter anyone. No one else had been in the tunnels. "They did this to your people? Hunted you?"

"Yes, they've hunted us beyond our capabilities of recovering as a solo species. It's why we've reached out. Otherwise, we will die out."

Damn. And the US had sold them on these intergalactic volunteer adventurers that were going to have sex with them and save their species? Did they care that I had arrived pregnant? …Was I?

I was lost in my worries when Zade stopped along a rock cliff which had a massive wooden door built into it. It had the vibes of an ancient portal in the middle of the wilderness. There was no house, no neighborhood, not even a street.

"You live in a cave?" No ticky-tacky here.

"Not all of us. Not even the prince will be as protected as you will be tonight," he said with an air of satisfaction.

We stepped into an entry with a few pairs of dusty coveralls hanging on a stand and boots of all the same size and wear along the wall. It seemed to serve as a mudroom, but weren't we in a cave? Lights glowed warmly from a large living space with a cooking area on one side. I knew I was in an alien's home, but I wasn't convinced he wasn't an alien in it too. I was expecting a sparsely decorated bachelor pad, but this house was many decades lived-in with small collections of trinkets and various rock collections.

"Was this your parents' home?"

"Yes, I'm the third generation. It was built by my grandfather and expanded by my father."

That explained it. Zade hadn't decorated this house. His family had. The furniture and sentimental items told stories that weren't his. Had he chosen not to redecorate, not had the time? He had at least cleaned. There were no layers of dust as I'd expect, especially for a cave.

"You will have the bigger bedroom," he said, opening a door from the living space.

He hadn't moved to his parents' bedroom. That sounded like laziness. He opened the door to the room. This room had been cleared of all knick-knacks. The furniture was pristine, new, and scaled for his human guest. The style was manufactured, bland, and clearly human. However, the effort to recreate human comforts in a Xavian cave was not lost on me. I'd entered many furnished bedrooms as a military brat, and I'd never appreciated one as I did now. My knees weakened.

"They provided a wide selection of clothes to start. If you need more of something, or something different, we will get it for you." He revealed several sets of clothes in a wardrobe.

Usually the sight of new clothes excited me, but my mind was reeling, and my body was quickly fading. The Xavians had put so much thought and care into hosting their guests. And my father was asking me to spy on them.

"I need to rest," I said, suddenly feeling like the room was spinning around me. I sat on the bed to make it stop.

"Sure, I will bring you something to eat and drink for when you are ready." Zade left, shutting me inside.

The mention of food didn't trigger any nausea symptoms. Should I be worried about that on top of everything else?

I laid down on the bed, which was much softer than I expected. The mattress came up and touched my ears like a pillow. It was much too soft. I froze mid-adjustment to an echo, a flutter, in my stomach. I'd never felt anything like it. I might not have even have believed it happened, except…it did again.

I wasn't alone.

Chapter Eleven
My Mystery Human

Zade

I left Cassie to settle into the room while I prepared the food I had promised. I thought she'd show more appreciation of the accommodations I was providing her. However, her mood turned, and I thought maybe she was hungry. I needed her to answer so many questions. Who was she? How did she know my name?

Impatient.

That's what my mother called me.

She also said I was just like my father.

She wasn't wrong. That's probably why we didn't get along well. She was upset that she had somehow raised a child just like his father. *Surprise.*

I needed to be careful. It was evident that Cassie was different than the other women. While she seemed the same age, she was shaped differently than the others. There was more to her. She had more curves and rolls. Her shadow had depth. She wasn't a sliver of a person. Her skin looked luxuriously soft. I longed to touch her round face, her cheeks reddening as we trekked home. She looked like she could enjoy our large cocks and survive a Xavian childbirth.

No, her extra level of strength and beauty was not by chance. She knew more than the others too. My name. She had interest in the mines. Was she sent to spy on me because I was the closest involved with the glor? That's what they cared about. They didn't care about Xavian politics or the Xavian prince. They needed Xavians because they needed glor.

I gathered water from the cavern system cleaned by the cliff's granite. I prepared a crunchy baked bread called brack and fruit from the nearby tree. I tapped on the door.

"Come in," she said.

I opened what still felt like my parents' bedroom door to the new reality of program-provided furniture and a program-provided mystery woman. She had changed from her space suit to much softer fabric that suited her and revealed more of the smooth skin along her neck and collarbone.

"Is there anything you need at the moment?" I asked, trying to be polite. I didn't know what a human fresh from stasis would need.

"I don't think I'm hungry." She sipped the water and frowned into it. Maybe she didn't know what she needed either.

"How did you know my name?"

Cassie giggled a bit. "Your photo is in the government pamphlets. I thought your piercing was hot. I asked your name. I didn't think I'd meet you so soon."

"Hot? It is not hot." I touched it to demonstrate.

Cassie's laughter broke my concentration. "I know. It can also mean *sexy* or *attractive*."

I smiled. She found my piercing attractive? It garnered discussion as it related to glor-minding, but I'd never heard someone think it…hot.

"Do you know any other Xavian names?" I quizzed her.

"None of the others had piercings." She pointed to the bridge of her own nose which was the tiniest round thing I'd ever seen pass as a nose. I wondered if she'd even be able smell milcress from milkweed.

"You know, my nose is pierced too." She tilted her head and pointed to the small hole.

"That's a hole? What fits in there?" I laughed. My piercing was much larger, rounder, through the bridge of my nose.

"A small hoop or a tiny stud."

"Who did you ask about my name?"

"One of the recruiters…I don't remember. There were so many people involved." She shook her head.

Something about her answer felt off, but I didn't know what. If she'd just overheard it, why not say that? She'd taken notice of my name, my piercing, and had asked about mining glor even as we ran from the Orkain. I'd never known anyone to be interested in any of those subjects besides my father. Why would she be?

"Do you know how long I was in stasis?" she asked.

How would I know that?

"They told us we were in stasis for three Earth months. How long between ships?"

"It's been seven rainy seasons since the first ship. The humans called it six months. So, it will be fourteen rainy seasons before they return if they do as they say…"

"What will I do until then?"

"You will stay with me or with another of the program hosts. I imagine Davian will be in communication with us shortly."

"Who is he?"

"Communications officer. Prince Drex will probably address the kingdom."

"Are Davian and the prince in the program too?"

"Davian, no. The prince, yes." This line of questions bothered me. Was she assessing potential targets? Was I not good enough for her?

Chapter Twelve
Dream Come True

Cassie

I was in my classic Cassie-is-falling dream, but suddenly Zade was at my side, pulling me in, rescuing me. I became aware of his body, hard against mine. His arms wrapped around me, chiseled pecs, abdominals, and those obliques. Christ, I wanted to be close to that body. I wanted to feel his skin. Was it like ours? Different? It looked silky. I want to run my fingers across his green muscles. Instead, I woke and ran them over my clit.

My body warmed quickly to my touch. I had become skilled with my fingers, copying my third favorite boyfriend's techniques. I'd become practiced after Colin threw out all of my vibrators. I thought he was OK with me having solo-play toys, but one day they were gone. My drawer was empty when I reached for one. I didn't even say anything to him about it. I just accepted it, like that was a normal way to communicate with someone. Fuck, that pissed me off. I should have been out of there a long time ago. Better late than never.

My brain had betrayed me; masturbating didn't feel great anymore. My buildup was an annoying pressure to relieve and upsetting my stomach. More annoying thoughts popped into my head. I angrily dismissed them, flipping around to gain more pressure on my hand. My face partially in the pillow, I breathed shallow and faster, and thought about dream-Zade on top of me. The orgasm came quick, sharp, then gone, pissing me off as much as it was supposed to relieve my stress.

I flipped over to ensure I cooled off. I didn't want to keep masturbating. If at first you don't succeed, cum, cum again, right? Not this time. More like, the definition of insanity is to repeat the same action expecting a different result.

What the fuck was I doing on this planet? My dad was gone. He didn't even stay to see if I survived the first hour. I didn't want to spy on Zade, but I might need to. Even if my father did return in a year, I would probably need to sell him information to get back on the ship. It was the smart thing to do, but it was also exactly what my father wanted me to do. I hated him for it.

To top it all off, I was horny and found this Zade-guy attractive. I couldn't have sex with him—only trouble could come of it, right? My boundaries weren't the greatest. My intergalactic blind date/host was the hottest man, alien, alien-man I'd ever seen. Not only was I afraid of getting caught as an outsider, I worried that Zade thought he'd gotten the fattest, ugliest woman of the bunch. Would he complain, especially if I didn't put out?

I assessed my body in the over-tall full-length mirror. I didn't have to pull up my night shirt to see my belly now or before the pregnancy. I examined my skin for stretch marks. None yet, but I wondered if Zade had anything like cocoa butter in his house. I tried not to think that it might be his mother's.

I'd never stayed with someone who lived in their dead parents' house before. I'd spent the night with guys who had lived with their parents—lots of drummers above garages or bassists in basements. I didn't stay long. I'd slip out of the house in the morning, doing the walk of shame past a mom with a cup of tea and a permanent eye roll.

Out of habit, I wondered what Zade's parents would think of me. They'd probably consider me a bad choice given my pregnancy and the fact that I was a different species than him. Well, at least I wouldn't have to worry about them.

I changed clothes. Given I'd never worn these before, I didn't know how much my body was changing. That was probably a good thing. Zade said he would pass on whatever didn't fit me, but I was afraid of my changing body. Who knew what I would need later? I sure as hell didn't. I wore loose pants with a Xavian version of a waistband and a flowy shirt before heading into the hallway.

Bad timing.

Zade opened the bathing room door. His hair was damp, glossy, and dark, dripping over his green bare chest. Holy shit. He was as hot as my dream. His slim body was framed with wicked obliques to a narrow V of abdominals. My breath caught in my throat.

"Hello," he said.

"Uh, good morning," I choked out.

"Is that what is customary? Uggood orning to you then." He gave his head a cute little awkward nod.

I only managed a cough. I wished for morning sickness in that moment. If I was nauseated, I wouldn't be feeling so embarrassed with deep rushes of desire running through me. I wouldn't be fucking horny and needy as hell. I wanted to throw myself on his freshly showered body and rub on him. Was that weird? Probably. I stepped closer to him. He smelled like lemon and hickory, but mostly I felt the heat emanating from him.

"You're warm," I said, alarmed.

He took my hand and dared put it on his tight pec. Zade was alien-hot in more ways than one.

"Wow," was all I could manage. I was gawking over this man's body.

My curiosity got the better of me, and I stepped closer. He responded to my presence too. His breath caught in his chest, and he didn't seem to be exhaling. He seemed a bit uncomfortable, and it felt nice to get the big guy on his heels for a moment. I had power. I stepped around him to the bathing room. He exhaled, shoulders dropping. I snuck a glimpse of his shapely ass in his towel. My knees felt weak, but I didn't grab that booty to catch myself. Instead, I went into the bathing room and closed the door before I did something stupid or passed out from my desperation.

I caught myself touching my breasts. I needed another rubdown. Why was I like this? It was easy to dismiss it as pregnancy hormones, but it made it difficult to ignore the ridiculously hot alien in a towel.

The bathing room had walls smoothed by water. In fact, it dripped down the walls as a natural feature. I worried the water would not be heated, but it was warm and piped to the ceiling to cascade like steady rain shower. The soap reminded me of Zade. The scent excited me, and I shivered.

But I couldn't have Zade.

Chapter Thirteen
Boundary

Zade

My sharp nose could smell Cassie's wet sex as soon as she entered the hallway. I didn't assume I consumed her thoughts as she pleasured herself—I sniffed again—with her fingers. However, I was emboldened to place her hand against my chest.

Her touch was electrifying. She walked off into the bathing room, abandoning me and my barely hidden arousal in the hall. My dicks fought the towel the entire way to my room. Cassie was beautiful, and I wanted not simply her hand on my chest but her entire body engulfing mine. Fryyre. No, what I needed was her out of my house as soon as possible. She was incredibly distracting.

Even if she was a spy, it felt disrespectful to touch myself with her across the hall. I didn't want to touch me. I wanted to touch *her*—her gorgeous curves invaded every single one of my thoughts. I tucked myself into pants and flexed the muscles in my thighs to redistribute the blood flow.

The settit signaled from my office. I was both relieved to receive communication and annoyed by the timing. I wrestled mentally to get my erection down while rushing to the call.

"Haellea, Zroso." I greeted Davian.

Davian was the communications officer, and of all the people in the government, the one I could most tolerate. He was near my father's age and had experience in the government both before and after the Orkain invasion. Now considered an elder, I wished he did more than communicate the wishes of inexperienced Prince Drex.

"Haellea" returned Davian. "Thank you for notifying us of Cassie's safety. Is she available to speak with me?"

"She just woke up and stepped into the bathing room. It is just as well. I need to speak with you. I don't want Cassie staying in my house."

The wrinkles deepened around Davian's furrowed brows and horns. "Cassie is in deep need. She was lied to by her government, trafficked to a foreign land, and needs shelter."

"I understand that, but maybe she could stay with another host." It was an easy solution. If Cassie needed to spy on me, I would make it impossible for her to do so.

"I'm not authorized to move anyone unless it is an emergency. Is it?"

"Well, no, it's not an emergency," I acquiesced. I didn't have proof, and even if I did, I could handle her for a time. Impatient.

"I will call back to speak with Cassie," Davian reported, leaving me to deal with my own problems, both immediate and otherwise.

I pumped my legs. This was simple sexual attraction. Anyone would be turned on by such a beautiful woman pleasing herself in one's bathing room. Still, the sooner Cassie was out of my house, the better.

Chapter Fourteen
Daylight

Cassie

I stepped out into the hallway and heard Zade speaking to someone. I didn't know who that someone was or what they were talking about, but Zade didn't sound happy. He was probably complaining about me. Maybe he was trying to trade me out. I didn't know what he was saying, but the sound of his dissatisfaction or unhappiness made me feel uneasy. Was this carpet going to fly out from underneath me too?

I tiptoed away. Perhaps it was the devil you knew, but it felt important to stay here with Zade. I already had to stay on this planet for a year. At the end, I didn't want to leave empty handed because I was moved early by Zade. If my baby and I were to survive this planet and the next, I would have to use and keep any advantage I could.

Zade wasn't the only one I would need to convince but he was a start. He was the only one I knew on this whole planet, except I guessed Layla now. My desire to know how she was doing helped me swallow my fears about leaving this room. So far, he'd minded my privacy, but it meant I needed to approach him.

Thankfully Zade was wearing more than a towel now. Slim-fitting clothes to not snag on rocks, I assumed, but it also looked good on him. He gave me a hot cup of tea as if it was a typical Thursday morning. Who knew? Maybe it was Thursday. I never could get the hang of Thursdays. The drink smelled spicy with hints of cherry. It was frightfully hot. He was halfway through his. Was this all we were going to eat this morning? I blew on mine. Zade stared at my lips.

I stopped.

"Do you have a way for me to communicate with Layla? I want to know if she is all right."

"I can call Moto." He clenched his jaw around Moto's name. I immediately caught on to some drama that wasn't my own.

"Who is he and why don't you like him?" I asked, cutting my eyes at Zade.

His gaze crossed over my face, trying to decipher how I'd figured it out. He must not have noticed how he said the dude's name.

"Moto is my neighbor. I don't have anything against him. It's just that proximity doesn't make for friendship."

"For me, it's the opposite. I moved around a lot when I was a kid, so I had to make friends with whoever was there. Then, out of sight, out of mind."

"Why did you move around a lot?" he asked.

"Oh, my dad's job." Damn. That was close. "So yeah, I don't know how to maintain a friendship or an enemy."

"We're not enemies."

"Did he bully you?" I asked. I don't know why. I guess it was the way he said he wasn't his enemy. Bully was the other school-age option.

"Yeah, he made sure everyone knew that he didn't like me. I don't know why. Guess to keep himself separate from me since we both lived in weird mine-caves."

I guess children's teasing was universal.

"I once got made fun of because I had an outie instead of an innie," I said sympathetically.

"What's that?" he asked.

"It's a different shape of your naval."

"Is it weird?" he asked. He stared down at my shirt.

"It's what it sounds like…more outside than inside…" I didn't want him to see my belly, but I also didn't want him imagining something gross on my stomach.

Not being good at explaining things, I lifted my shirt to show my naval. It seemed to be protruding even more than usual. I counted two whole seconds before yanking my shirt down.

"And 'made fun of' means they teased you?" he asked, making sure he got things straight.

I nodded.

"I can see why. It's so small." He grimaced.

"That's not why they teased me…but, wait. It doesn't sound nice the way you're saying it either. Is my belly button not acceptable here either?"

"I'm teasing you." He flashed his perfect smile at me again and I was reminded of shining diamonds. He gestured for me to follow him.

I considered stewing, because he was being a jerk. But I did want to talk to Layla, so I followed down the hall to a thick, dry wooden door. It creaked open, scraping the stone floor with its sagging weight. The lights turned on automatically over the space and over a stone desk feature. Books filled the walls. His entire house was like real-life Flintstones, using natural rockface as furniture while incorporating technology.

Were they more advanced than we were on Earth? It was difficult to compare from an individual Xavian's things. We obviously had different needs as a people and as a culture. Although, Zade was one of few who lived in caves, I thought. His grandfather built this place not far from the mines. It seemed mining was a family tradition, and more prestigious. And I'd shown the dude my naval.

Zade pressed on the mirror-like device on the desk. "This is a settit. It transmits real-time video to other settits."

Moto answered and greeted us. He was objectively handsome, symmetric with a square jaw and thick horns. He was broader and more jock-like than Zade, and I could imagine him intimidating Zade when they were younger. Zade, with his purple-silver hair looked more like the lead singer in a rock band. Moto was the muscular athlete.

"Cassie wanted to speak with the human guest, Layla," Zade didn't bother with a greeting.

"It's a pleasure to see you again, Cassie."

He gave a little bow of his head. I pretended to enjoy his politeness to annoy Zade. "I will go see about Layla for you." He walked out of the frame and, I presume, from the room.

"I can handle this part on my own." I made a shooing gesture.

"I don't think that's necessary," Zade seemed reluctant to leave. He observed my shooing gesture as a strange motion. I guess it was.

"Please, I'd like some privacy."

He left, but he did not close the door behind him. It was too heavy to not draw attention to me closing it either. I rolled my eyes.

Even when we were running for our lives yesterday, I'd noticed how gorgeous Layla was. Now was no different. Her brown hair curled perfectly around a pristine face with dark eyes and a long nose that matured her doll-like features. She was the sort of pretty that immediately put me on guard. I wanted to find fault with her. She was probably mean. She probably didn't like me, just like Moto didn't like Zade. But it wasn't like that at all. Her face lit into a wide smile, brightening at the sight of me. I couldn't help but return the smile. Tears welled up in the corners of her cheeks. She approached the settit and gently blocked Moto from the frame. I was crying a little too.

"I'm glad you made it all right," said Layla. "Did you hear about the one woman?"

I shook my head.

"Davian said she hid in the ship and was pulled out by the Orkain. He said she's dead."

"What's Davian like?"

"Oh, he really sympathetic. If you haven't talked to him yet, then you will soon. He's calling all of us."

"What kind of questions did he ask?"

"Oh, just what we were told, if we needed anything. I don't know."

"What did happen to us?" I asked. "What's your story?"

"I was the accountant who went viral on TikTok. Got picked, took a sabbatical from my job, and woke up here." Her eyes took on a glassy, distant look.

"They'll be back for us," I reassured her. I felt bad for her. "There's a lot of money involved."

"What? I mean…Yeah, I spent a lot of money on creating my web content, editing and my make-up, but I didn't give them any money. Did you? Was this a scam?" she asked.

Oh no, I was already messing up. "No, no, I don't think so. I meant like… the government spent a lot of money to bring us here. If they want more of that rare earth metal, they'll be back. Were you a web-influencer or something back home?" I asked.

"No, no, I really was an accountant. Very much the opposite, just entered the contest and won! At least, I think I won…"

"Same," I lied. "Not about the accountant part. I was…uh, between jobs."

"I work for a company out in the Midwest that allows you a sabbatical, so I applied for that."

"That's pretty neat. You'll still have a job if you go back."

"Yeah, back…to Wisconsin to be an accountant? No way I'm going back there."

It's not like I had much to go back to either. I shrugged. She picked at a string on her shirt.

"So, Moto's a nice guy?" I asked in girl-code language. Zade was annoying, but he wasn't dangerous. It wasn't only Zade's warning about Moto…the guy wasn't my type. Too heavy and thick and dumb-looking. I preferred Zade's slender rock-star frame to Moto's line-backer build.

"Yeah, he seems nice enough," she said, which I understood in girl-talk as meaning, "He hasn't tried anything but I haven't put my guard down yet."

"I don't think mine wants me to stay," I said. I glanced at the open door. Could he hear me from out there? Did Xavians have good hearing?

"Because of your pregnancy?" she whispered.

My jaw dropped. "How diyya—?" I suddenly regretted speaking with Layla.

"Don't worry. You're not really showing. I come from a really big family, so I notice *things*. I mean, I'm sorry, that's probably weird to say. At least you knew... That one girl I told once..."

"No, I don't think he knows. I don't even know how far along I am because of the stasis."

"How far along were you before?"

"Maybe a couple of months? And we spent three months in stasis and I think we aged some in there..." I was rambling, but I was so glad to be able to go over the math with someone else. I didn't know how stasis worked; I had no idea when I was due.

"Do you think they'd believe it's one of theirs if you...you know?"

My eyebrows rose. Layla wasn't a naïve Midwestern accountant. She also had a good idea. At least until the birth, that might keep me and my baby protected.

"Stay safe."

"Right," I muttered.

"Congratulations. You're going to be like the first human to give birth on Xavia. And they are going to be the first human Xavian." Layla's face had a bright glow.

I wasn't sure what was going to happen to me when it became evident that I was *with child*. But I did feel surprisingly better now that someone else knew. Even though my dad had dumped me, I hadn't faded into limbo. I wasn't at risk of disappearing completely into the ether just yet. "Thank you. I'm scared."

"Of course you are, but you have a friend in me."

No one had ever so quickly declared friendship with me. I was thankful for it but wasn't sure how long it would last. Would she be my friend if she knew my father was the one who dropped her off like cattle? Or that I hadn't been tricked like her?

Oh well. I needed a friend, even if it was only going to be until the truth came out.

Chapter Fifteen
Mine

Zade

Cassie was still on the settit with Layla, and I was getting antsy. The morning was late, and I hadn't left for the mines yet. I know Davian and the rest of the program wanted me hosting my guest, but how was I going to do that and keep the mines operational?

I heard the settit's notification. There was another call. I approached the office. Cassie was already done with her conversation with Layla and was walking around the office. How long had she been off the settit? I hadn't wanted to leave her alone in here, but I didn't have time to be annoyed because Bern was calling.

"It's work," I said to Cassie. She took my hint and gave me the same privacy I afforded her. She left the office, and I was left wondering what she'd been doing in here for how long.

I answered the settit. "What is it?" Whatever it was was my fault because I should have been in the mines this morning.

"The results for the latest tests have finished and are waiting to be reviewed."

"When did that happen?"

"Earlier this morning. I, uh, expected you in, so I paused operations."

"You did what?" My heart pounded in my chest. Nothing. Nothing had been done all day. This was ridiculous and exactly why I needed to be in the mines every day. I didn't have time to host a woman, especially one from which I needed to guard my position.

I stormed from the room. I didn't even care if Bern turned the machines on at this point. I would rather be at the mine. There was already so much that had been potentially lost.

Cassie was in the main living space on the urish. Her eyes widened at the sight of me. I honestly didn't have time to concern myself with her fear, fake or otherwise.

"I have to go to the mines." I put on my boots.

"Oh, should I go with you?" she asked as she worked herself out of the soft urish.

"No." I didn't want her at the mines gathering intelligence. "Davian the communications officer is supposed to talk with you today. You touch the screen when he is calling to connect. Otherwise, I don't want you in my office. Or my bedroom. Also, don't leave the cave. It's dangerous."

"You're leaving the cave," she replied coolly.

"It's dangerous for me too. But I have familiarity. You will get lost."

Cassie's lips pursed, but she didn't argue. Was she just being contrary?

After a quick glance to the skies, I slipped out the door and escaped to the mines.

Chapter Sixteen
Sneaking

Cassie

Whatever was happening at the mine must have been important, because the dude left me in his house. If he thought a rushed rule to not enter his space was enough to keep me out of it…it wasn't. I needed to know who I was dealing with. After waiting in the living room to make sure he had left, I ventured to the office. The door was heavy and sagged. It scraped loudly across the stone floor.

I ran my fingers on the cool, smooth stone surface of the desk. It had been carved from the cave itself. It jutted from the wall, a permanent piece of furniture. It had seen generations of use, worn in places where Zade's forefathers had rested their wrists and hands. To the side were stacks of rolled papers. I unfurled a few. One was a schematic for a machine. The others were more like maps, possibly of the mines—a treasure trove for my father. How would I collect this information though? My father hadn't packed me a camera, nor had I spotted a giant office-gray copy/fax machine in this room. He'd notice if too much went missing. I'd have to hand-copy this stuff…trace it maybe. That could take a while, but it wasn't like I didn't have the time. Well, until the baby arrived.

I pulled open a drawer. Maybe there would be some spare drafting paper, writing utensils, or some fun secrets. Who knew what men kept in their desks?

A lot of junk, apparently.

However, there was a faded photo stuck to the bottom of the drawer. I gently peeled it up. At first I thought it was Zade with a child, but then I realized Zade *was* the child. He didn't yet have his piercing, but his father did. They had the same long purple hair. Like father, like son. Zade fell into his father's footsteps so well, I suspected this was still more his father's office than his own. Zade wasn't in the military, but he had conformed into a convincing replica of his father.

I pulled a dusty tome of a book from the shelf and cracked it open. Fortunately, the chair was made of a softer material than rock. I plopped into it with my legs hanging over the arm of the massive wingback throne and flipped through the pages. Their written language had round looping symbols. It was oriented vertically and as they say, it was all Greek…or Xavian to me. Even the illustrations were a mystery.

Still, I was feeling pretty badass. That is, until I heard Zade calling my name from the living room. Shit. I jumped from the seat and returned the book. Even if he hadn't seen the open office door yet, he'd catch me leaving. I was trapped.

Chapter Seventeen
Catching Her

Zade

Bern was smart enough to restart the mining operations by the time I had arrived. He had also performed all of the next checks, but I went over them again. I didn't trust that things had been done correctly unless I had seen them with my own eyes. I went to each station with the unread tests in my hand to gather the results myself.

It didn't matter that I'd gathered them myself. They were still unfavorable. Bern had an argument for pausing operations. If it was a fresh site, we would never dig in these locations. It's just where the equipment already was. I worried we needed to relocate. I established new survey locations. I had Bern set up the initial tests. I could come back and review them afterward.

For now, I needed to return and check on Cassie. I'd left her alone in that house and my office. I didn't keep much in there, but my father had. Sure, it was in another language, but I still didn't trust it in her hands. It was information valuable to glor mining and thus valuable to the humans. Maybe I could catch her in the act of going through the office. Then I would have other proof besides her knowing my name.

I was out of breath when I got to the door to my cave, whether it was from nearly running here or my panic, I wasn't sure. I leaned an arm on the door frame and caught my breath, before quietly opening the door. She wasn't in the main living space, thankfully. I realized it was probably improper to be attempting to surprise a woman who was supposed to be my guest.

"Cassie? I forgot something," I claimed from down the hallway. I watched the other doors, but I already saw that my office door was open.

"Good," she called, not hiding that she was in my office. I had her.

I almost staggered out of the room backward when I turned the corner and saw her splayed out on my desk.

Her bare feet were pointed atop my paperwork. Her knees bent and open with her skirt bunched between her legs.

I was expecting her elbows to be deep in rolls of paper, surprised. I was not expecting this.

"I'm so glad you're back."

My eyes followed the lines of her legs from her toes to her knees to her pillowy thighs that disappeared into the bunches of cloth. Something about seeing her foreign skin against our Xavian cloth materials felt vulgar. I yearned to yank the fabrics off her body. I wanted to see what curves our voluminous clothing was covering. I stepped over to the desk, protective of it. I was supposed to be, right? It allowed me to get close to her. Her warm skin emanated soaff interacting with her skin's chemistry. I could almost taste it on the air. I wanted to taste it on her skin. But this wasn't time to get distracted.

"What are you doing in here?"

"Snooping," was her one-word answer.

I didn't know that term. "Snooping?"

"Going through someone's stuff to find out about them."

There was the confession of her crime…the crime of snooping. I was excited that she might want to learn more about me. However, I suspected she only cared about glor. "What did you find out?" I asked.

"I'm not sure what I've found out about you…and what I've found out about your father."

I tensed, suddenly again in my father's shadow as if he loomed. He wasn't, and she'd never met him, but I had been here many times before. She wasn't on my desk. She was on his. I no longer felt possessive of it. Despite not knowing our language, she was perceptive. She was here for whoever had access to the glor—not specifically me. She didn't want me to return home.

I would challenge this bluff. I stepped between her open legs, against the desk. I leaned over her. Any moment she would crawl out from under me, jump out of my reach, weirded out by the alien that leered over her. I would make her regret her ploy to distract me.

My face was inches above hers.

She didn't flinch, but she did tense.

She remained rigid underneath me. This is where she got scared and fled. To make sure she knew I was serious, I lowered closer. Her hands slipped on the papers underneath her. I caught her head in my hand. Her golden hair felt silky smooth and finer than I imagined.

Did humans kiss? I secretly hoped not. I grinned at the thought. She'd be even more freaked out when our lips touched.

And then her lips captured mine. I'd been playing the aggressor, but I was shocked by the outcome and just how soft her lips were. If anything, shock kept me there—that and her hands pulling at my shirt collar. How far would she go to keep me from asking questions? She was only delaying the inevitable. Still, I was an amused and willing participant.

Her body was soft. Everywhere. From this position, it was easy to imagine shooting my seed inside her. Her stomach and breasts would grow even larger—her whole body changing because of me. Surely the government would say I'd done my duty. I could discover why she was snooping…later.

Chapter Eighteen
Seducing Him

Cassie

Oh shit.

What the hell was I doing? The fear I felt when he caught me in his office had my heart racing. I hadn't thought this through when I jumped on the desk. I was kissing this alien. Albeit, the finest-muscled person I'd ever kissed, but an alien all the same. Layla's suggestion burned in the back of my mind. Laying this alien could buy me some time. I couldn't go through with that, could I?

From what I understood, it was Zade's job to seduce and mate me. I was just making it easy for him. I didn't know his intentions but he seemed accepting of me, or at least my body. There were a dozen reasons to do this. It wouldn't be the worst decision I'd made this year—hell, it might not even rank at year's end.

Zade's lips were velvet-soft. Was his tongue? I entered his mouth and met guarding teeth. I wasn't yet deterred. Perhaps there were no "French" Xavians to teach him this tradition. I wanted more of him, my tongue searching for his, but he wouldn't give. My body felt like it was melting underneath him. Not a slow thaw of ice either, but of heated, bubbling wax in his hand and against his lips. He leaned heavily on me, unafraid of hurting me or possibly not caring. His fingers greedily clawed the rough fabric on my hip. I forgot about the French as electricity spiked through my side, fiery warmth and desire filling me. I ran my fingers through his hair, hardly making a slow approach to the horn on that side. His top lip lurched when I caressed the slim horn. It was sensitive. I slowed my touch. It was smooth like antler trophies I dared touch in my grandfather's den. A rumble seemed to emanate from his core. A growl, a purr? It turned me up another notch. I shoved my tongue back into his mouth. This time his teeth parted and…

Wow.

What was going on in his mouth? It was like making out with more than one person…more than one tongue. I searched with my own, feeling him out, him feeling me out. I couldn't discern the exact anatomy. His tongue moved above and below mine, hot, intense, and intimate. I was losing my sense of time and reason in my exploration of him. All that I had fought back this morning rushed back between my legs with a vengeance.

Zade moved his hand from my hip to my neck. His other cradling the entire back of my head. That fear flashed forward again. I felt vulnerable, very much aware of our size difference. He could overpower me. And still, I wanted to continue, risk what would happen. My fingers wandered down his silvery hair onto his neck, which tensed underneath my touch. Muscles lengthened and bulged, and I followed them down to the pluck of his collar bone and the chiseled dip of his shoulder and chest. I pulled on the string tie on the neck of his shirt and loosened the knot, pulling his shirt collar open.

Was I going to regret this? Perhaps I wasn't a bad spy after all. He seemed to have forgotten that he had caught me red-handed in his office. I batted my eyelashes and now we were making out and wrinkling precious schematics as he climbed onto the desk with me. Things clattered to the stone floor below us. A heavy and thick leg fell between my legs. His cock flinched close to my knee. My eyes must have revealed my surprise; all that extra geometry tutoring my father paid for in high school finally culminating to this *Oh Shit* moment. And just as instantaneously, he had pulled off of me. Entirely. Like he was going to deny me.

"This room is off limits." He had taken his hands and lips from my body but he remained close against the table.

I took the opportunity to wipe a bit of moisture off the edge of my lip from our passionate kiss. I was a little love drunk and a little annoyed that he'd put on the brakes. It made me look desperate. I guess I was.

"I'm sorry. How can I make it up to you?" I swung my legs around and underneath me, crushing rolled papers. I stared into his bright spiraling eyes, which felt more alien than his horns or his turquoise skin. They had to work differently than ours, the way the colors inside swirled, and yet I felt like I understood his expressions. We weren't that different... And he was struggling to deny me.

I didn't try to kiss him again. My hands and fingers caressed his collarbone, his pecs, working my way slowly down his tense, still body. I followed the muscles of his abdomen, tight ripples of skin and strength to the V, slipping my fingers underneath the fabric.

"I want to touch you." Forget holmium. There were more pressing matters in the moment. What was in these shorts?

I'd reached inside to the base of his thick shaft. My eyes widened when my thumb couldn't find my fingers. When I pulled my hand toward me, it was not a smooth single length either. The sensation felt familiar but I couldn't place it until Zade stuck his three tongues out at me as a visual cue. His eyes glinted with mischief and anticipation, bolstered by my stunned expression.

Zade had three dicks. Yeah, forget the galaxy spinning eyes. *The three dicks* were probably the most alien thing about him.

Pre-cum, or whatever Xavians have, came from multiple places with my stroke. His smile grew, his eyes oscillating lazily as I moved my hand to explore him.

His three cocks were wrapped around each other, separated in my hands and moved individually from his base. Like his tongues, they were prehensile. They twisted and extended in my hand. He gave a bit of a shudder, and I paused. I didn't know what sort of pacing was required to please an alien, but I wanted to take it slow and needed him to cum inside me. I pulled my hand out of his pants and a velvety blue-green cock followed, rising upward. Fuck, how would it feel to have that inside me? I was about to find out. I was about to go where no human woman had gone before.

I yanked on his waistband before leaning back onto my ass, inviting him on top of me. I pulled my panties down and could feel his eyes studying my cunt. When he undid his pants and pushed them over his hips, I didn't look down. I couldn't chance getting scared or grossed out. I needed to finish the deed no matter how weird shit got. Still, I was undeniably excited when I reached with my fingers for his closest shaft. I looked into his eyes as I guided him into my wet pussy.

Pressure blossomed into pleasure as I adjusted to his girth. I was enjoying myself and even dropped a hand down to massage another shaft. I pressed it greedily to my clit.

I tensed when his other head pushed on my already full pussy. I couldn't imagine more in there.

He whispered in my ear. "Oh, my sweet thing, relax. Let's double the chance I give you a child. Let me fill that pretty hole."

My plan was working out better than I anticipated. He wanted to give me a child. I couldn't resist acting out the scenario. I was undeniably turned on by his request. I took a deep breath and willed my thighs to spread outward as he stretched me to my limits. I shuddered as he expanded and pulsed inside me, my channel clenching. My fingers dug into the taut skin on his shoulders. My eyes rolled back as his rhythm became erratic and fast.

"Cum inside me. Ohh, cum." I lost what I was saying as his pleasure rolled through me. He grunted and jets of pearly cum squirted over my clothed chest. More pumps inside and out.

I came too. It was impossible not to. He was everything my pussy needed in triplicate. The post-nut clarity was intense though. I'd performed an intimate act with an alien…what was protocol after this?

I didn't have to wonder for long. Zade pulled two cocks slowly out of me, slick with our cum. He dismounted me, and gently pushed me back down when I tried to get up. "Lay still," he commanded.

I obeyed. He wiped the cum from my skin, and pressed it into my slit like none could be wasted. If I wasn't laying him to plant the thought of pregnancy in his mind already, I'd be offended. As it was, I was in awe and surprisingly turned on by his measures. He wanted me pregnant. Then he was at my feet, threading my panties back on, pulling them up my legs. I helped get them over my ass. I'd never been dressed after a fucking. No one had ever been so deliberate to impregnate me either.

"You can leave now," he said as he fastened his pants. He looked me directly, daring me to say something. Some body language was universal.

My breath felt thick in my chest and my heart fluttered. On one hand, I wasn't being questioned about my trespass. On the other… Who did I just have sex with?

Zade stepped away with his arms across his chest. My confusion swung to annoyance as he didn't even bother to help me off the desk. I clambered off to one side, hot with embarrassment.

"What the hell?" I fumed, not even sure why I was mad or if I should be. I felt like a child being scolded and rejected.

"This room is off limits," he said, his voice as cold as the stone around us. The darker green left his cheeks.

The mood had changed so quickly. I was full of his seed and being shooed from the room. I felt used and gross. I went to the bathing room to maybe wash some of my stupidity and shame off. At least the deed was done. I cleaned myself with tears and shower water.

Chapter Nineteen
A Spy

Zade

Well, that had gotten out of hand. I rushed her from the room so I could think for a moment. My heart threatened to beat out of my chest, and my cock threatened to burst from my pants. Her scent was still thick in the air. I'd given into temptation, melted at her syrupy sweet words. She was probably laughing inwardly over how quickly I'd orgasmed but… Wow, was she tight. I was already ready to go again, and I wanted to do it right, but no—I needed to clear my head.

I picked up things I'd strewn from the desk onto the floor in my desperate need to touch her body. I was such a sucker. What trouble had I gotten myself into? Maybe I could figure out what she had been looking at before I arrived and messed this all up. How much evidence would Davian need? And how much had I ruined by having sex with the enemy?

I pressed buttons on the settit which sat on my desk. Communication devices of its size were typically portable, but the density of the cave walls required the device to be connected to the electrical system. Catching my appearance on the screen's reflection, I retied my shirt and ran my hand through my hair.

"Haellea," Davian greeted me, his face appearing on the screen. He was the communications officer and one of our eldest working closely with the prince. His horns were darkened and twisted with age.

"Haellea. I caught the woman in my office. She isn't who she's pretending to be."

Davian squinted. He had as many wrinkles as ridges. "How long did you leave her unattended?"

"Not long. I had to go to the mines, but I was suspicious. I returned to find her in my office, which I had deemed off limits."

"And what have you done with her?" He asked, eyebrows raised in accusation.

"Uh, nothing." Nothing like that. This wasn't going as I expected. "I reminded her the office was off limits and she left the room."

"Well, perhaps it's just a misunderstanding then. It's not like she can read our language. Remember, she was abandoned on a strange planet. She is scared."

I thought about Cassie splayed *unabandoned* on the desk. "I don't think that *scared* describes her." Could Davian see the mussed items and see where that big, gorgeous butt had been planted? No, of course not. I moved a few things around anyway. "Maybe she knows more Xavian than the others. Did any of the other women know alien names or even a word of our language?"

"Well, no." Davian paused. "They don't seem to know much, but they all had seen photographs of us. Maybe she recognized your piercing and was given your name."

I didn't want to admit that's what she said. "Still—why was she in my office, looking at information on the glor mines?"

"Stop. They don't know our language. She didn't know what she was looking at." Then, more directly, "You need to stop thinking she's some kind of…spy."

"I'm not really certain she's a victim either."

"Of course she is!" Davian said angrily.

"None of the other women seem suspicious? Who is with Prince Drex or Vance?" I hated to bring up Vance, but his role was significant in our government.

"Sisters—Katy and Sara. Lovely, scared women getting to know their hosts. And those two would have been targets before you."

Actually, the probability of sisters snagging the top two hosts seemed suspicious to me, but I wasn't going to convince him of that. He was too focused on in-politics to consider that outsiders might consider my position more important. I had to do the right thing here. "I don't think Cassie should stay with me."

"What? You haven't given this enough time. Stay home and get to know your guest. There are no problems with the glor production, I would hope."

I didn't want to get into that with him. "I am needed there—and I don't see anything wrong with safeguarding our most coveted resource from the humans."

"Don't think of them as 'the humans.' If all works out, our world is going to look a lot more human. They are us and she could possibly be your mate. Where is Cassie? I need to speak with her. Can you bring her in?"

My mate? As if. "Right now?" I gawked.

"Yes. I will wait this time."

Whatever patience he had with me was waning. I didn't have much time left to convince him. Perhaps Cassie would do it on her own. If she confessed, Davian would have to remove her from my place. Then things could go back to normal.

Chapter Twenty
Meeting Davian

Cassie

The heavy slap of the cave wall in lieu of a knock startled me. My heart jumped into my throat and buzzed like a bee. I couldn't discern individual beats, much less slow it down.

"Davian is on the settit. You are to explain what you were doing in my office."

"You ratted on me?" I stood, though the height difference remained.

"Ratted?"

"Tattled. Told on me. I wasn't even doing anything. You don't know how much trouble you've made." Or maybe he did. I didn't know the rules on Xavia.

"You act as if I did something wrong."

My skin prickled with my blood nearly boiling underneath. "In my culture, we don't get other people involved in our business."

"This is Xavian business. I involved the communications officer," he explained. He didn't seem to understand or care to understand.

"In my culture, we attempt to communicate with the person before involving a communications officer. There's like a basic trust—"

"—that we don't have." Zade interrupted me. "I did communicate with you. I told you not to go in my office."

I guessed he was right. We didn't have any foundation of trust. I'd been caught doing something I shouldn't have been. I had broken that basic trust. Even in my culture, it was probably best to give me up to the government and let them deal with me.

I sat down on the bed. I sank much farther than I expected, much like my heart. What if they thought I was copacetic in the intergalactic trafficking scheme? That was possibly a major crime. Could I go to whatever their form of prison was? This was ridiculous. He had to know this was ridiculous.

"Am I in trouble?" I asked.

"That depends." He leaned back, pleased.

"Depends on what?" There was no way in hell I was having sex with him again. I didn't care how hot he was. I wasn't like that.

"Depends on if you are honest with us. This is could be considered a Xavian-human misunderstanding, or maybe we'll have to punish you and keep you isolated."

"Then why did you have sex with me?" Now he was playing by the rules?

"That's the purpose of the hosting program. If given the opportunity, extend Xavian genetic lines."

Oh, he had a point. Maybe I hadn't thought it all through. "I don't even understand your written language," I pleaded.

"So you say. Then why were you in my office?" His eyes widen as he waited impatiently for my answer. He'd had that same greedy look when he had kissed me. I ignored a dark urge to kiss him…or stab him. If I didn't think clearly and struggled to give him a good answer, I might end up struggling to explain in front of a court next. I wouldn't have known his name or even cared to step foot in this office if my dad hadn't given me the idea. I needed to deflect—anything to get him off my case.

"I told you, I'm just nosey. I wanted to know more about you and Xavia. I was bored and I couldn't go outside because one of those monsters might attack me. But now, I'm being hassled by you and it's scaring me." I threw up my hands, but I had nowhere to go.

"I don't believe you," he said. "Let's go speak with Davian."

Damn it.

He escorted me across the hall, and I couldn't help but pause for a moment outside the threshold. I slipped into a smile. "May I?"

He rolled his head toward the threshold in what I expect is the Xavian equivalent to rolling their eyes. I made a show of stepping across and looking around as if I was going to be struck dead for entering the room.

"Sit at the desk, not on it," he said quietly.

Touché.

The desk had been neatened and basically emptied. Everything had been stashed away from my "human spy" eyes. If anything was damaged when he knocked his belongings off the desk when we were making out, it was not my fault. I had forgotten about the settit. Had it recorded any of my snooping or of us having sex?

I didn't recognize the face of the male Xavian that graced the surface. Of course, they'd all towered over me, and we had been in a bit of a hurry. Now I looked straight on, which I'd never do in any other circumstance. It gave me a bit of confidence, as did his kind face. He had a gentle smile and looked older than Zade, closer to Zade's father's age in the last of the photographs around the house.

"Hello, Cassie," said the man serenely. "I'm Davian."

It felt weird to have such a stately man not use my full legal name, but maybe they didn't have surnames here. I was no longer on Earth, and this wasn't the U.S. Government…thankfully. The Xavians only knew me as Cassie because that's the name I had given Zade. I could be anyone here. I was Cassie here, not Cassiopeia Smith. Cassiopeia Smith had the baggage of her parents and of Colin.

"First, Prince Drex and the Xavian kingdom acknowledge our significant part in your situation. You understood this as a visit to experience our culture, not to necessarily become a part of it. While the humans misrepresented the truth to both of us, you are our guests and free to leave if the means become available. We also apologize for your loss during the Orkain attack."

"My loss? What happened?" I asked, playing dumb. Maybe I could gain Davian's favor if he thought I had no idea what was going on.

"One of your comrades was abducted by the Orkain after she did not evacuate the ship."

"She's dead? What was her name?" Layla hadn't known. Maybe one of the other women had.

"We don't know. I'm not sure how much blood your species can lose…"

I thought about that *thing* taking off with a woman. I started to feel sick. "Is that a common occurrence?"

"Unfortunately, yes. That is why we were working with the humans to bolster our population and rebuild our species. However, we are not in the business of 'trafficking.' Once again, we are regretful that our choices allowed for your situation. Here, you are our guests with the rights of any Xavian until a time that a ship returns for you. Given their deception, we would understand and support any decision you make regarding your return."

I swallowed, trying to digest all that he was saying. While my dad and the government had dumped us to be wombs for these aliens, it turns out the Xavians weren't as barbaric as humans were. I also noted he hadn't accused me of being a spy. I wasn't going to bring it up. I had my part to play.

"Do you think they'll return?"

Davian hesitated. "We do think they'll return as long as they want more holmium from us. You are familiar with the material?"

That's what Zade had said. "Not intimately, no. You call it glor?"

"Yes, it was the resource we traded for…this opportunity. We apologize again for our part in your plight. Is there anything you need? Do you want to stay with Zade?"

I wasn't expecting this. I smiled sheepishly. My neck was hot and red. Inwardly, I burned. Zade had set me up. This call had nothing to do with me being in his office. What could I ask for that would put Zade in a bad light? I wanted him to feel as uncomfortable as I had felt.

"I feel confined in this cave. I'm not even allowed to be in all of it."

"Is that so? Well, perhaps there is information of a sensitive nature that needs to be kept confidential. I can ask that Zade remove anything of that nature so that you may have access to the entirety of the cave. Zade and his family have an unusual house. However, it has proven to be one of the safest in design, and many of our new houses have been built with that one in mind, although not always as part of a cave."

"Perhaps we don't have to tell her so much, Zroso." Zade said behind me.

Did Zade not want me to know these things? Was parentage as embarrassing to bachelors on Xavia as it was on Earth? Davian apparently did not think this information needed to be confidential. I didn't know what the word Zroso meant. Maybe it was Davian's last name or some sign of respect. It seemed to temper the delivery of Zade's statement, making it more palatable to Davian.

"Is there anything else you need?" Davian asked.

"No, that'll be it for now. I'm grateful for Zade's hospitality."

After we disconnected, I could see Zade and me together in the reflection.

"That was a cruel thing to do," I said. I launched from the chair with such force that I expected it to topple behind me and stormed from the room before he could tell me it was off limits again.

Zade was an asshole.

Chapter Twenty-One
Long Shot

Zade

It was a long shot to hope that putting those ideas in Cassie's mind would cause her to mess up. Davian was too good about letting them all play the victim. I mean, yes, most of them were victims, sure. But not this one. Not Cassie. Cassie knew something that the others didn't know. And it was going to bother me until I figured out what.

How did she know my name?

I mulled over the thought as I gathered everything sensitive about the glor mines…which was basically everything in the office. At least I was here to protect it. Davian would have her sleeping in this room if she requested. If it meant leaving the mines without his watchful eyes, then so be it.

It was time I cleaned out my father's office anyway. They had offered to do so when they set up Cassie's room with human-sized furniture. They'd mentioned it would be a good third bedroom for a big family. I couldn't imagine the place with little ones running around, fuller than when I was the child.

I couldn't imagine it because my father had spent most of his time in the mines…like I did now. And I didn't have nearly as much to show for it. I was grasping at wisps and wishes of glor. Perhaps it would do me some good to spend some time away. My senses were being dulled. Leaving the mines would mean that little would get done, but if I came back and was able to lead us to a new vein of glor…well, that would be worth it in the end. I had to keep the current struggle quiet from those who desperately wanted that knowledge. Not only Cassie and the humans, but Vance was always looking for an excuse to get rid of the whole industry of glor. It was as if he didn't understand it and had no personal need for it, so it could easily be done away with.

Nothing was that simple. He was an idiot.

#

A few solars later, the dry heat of the mine felt welcoming, more like home than the cavern with Cassie in it a short distance away. I had spent time in the mines as a child. My own would not. They could explore the caves possibly as they grew older but not where Xavians had dug greedily. I approached an example of this carelessness in the office door, which often stuck depending on the environmental humidity.

Unable to juggle the boxes and fight the door, I set down all the documents I'd taken from my home office. I had more to bring on a second trip. After unlocking and unsticking the door, I found the entire room to be dark. Bern must be running late.

No, it was more than that. The interior lights warmed and presented a darkened control board. It had been powered off, which hadn't been done since my father's death. After his funeral, I turned everything back on, and it'd been on ever since. I'd taken over for him.

Now the monitors were blank and not even an error light flashed. All operations had been turned off. What the hell had happened while I was gone? Did everyone decide to go home and ignore their jobs? I powered on the control board, ran diagnostics, and opened records. My foreman had turned off glor operations the day I caught Cassie in my office. It had been two solars since then, two solars with everything shut off.

I called Bern, the foreman.

"Haellea, are we back working?" Bern asked with a happy smile when he saw I was at the mines.

"What do you mean? You aren't working at all!" I shouted, partly because I was some distance from the settit, but mostly because I was angry.

"Aye, Vance told me to halt mining operations while you were getting your human guest settled. Have you already performed your duty of impregnation?"

"Vance?" I stormed to the settit for confirmation.

"Of course. Who else would I shut down the mine for? I assumed it was Prince's orders or yours."

I saw green. Vance had shut down operations behind my back. Bern apologized, and I turned off the settit because I didn't need it to record my string of profanities. He would be on his way.

Vance had pulled stuff like this before. He would get away with it. He would claim a miscommunication and Drex would believe him. It was power games and other immature crap. How did we survive with a naïve prince and his goofball adviser? Things would be run differently if I had authority outside of these mines.

I didn't even have that. Drex or Vance could shut me down as soon as they deemed it unnecessary. So many industries had already been scaled back or shut down. The needs of our smaller population had changed. Glor mining was only as valuable as the humans found it valuable. Did Vance and Drex not need more women?

We were solars behind because I could not be everywhere at once. I crashed my forearm into the top box of the items I'd lugged here. It flew across the room. No one else cared about me clearing my sensitive documents out of the office. Vance didn't think the industry was worth keeping, much less protecting. He should be working to kill the Orkain, not subverting my mining operation so he can dig tunnels from home to home like we were rodents.

The control board lit partially, requiring several physical check-offs for the processing chain to restart. Bern would be calling in the crew, but I wasn't one to wait. By the time they arrived, everything would be started. I knew every station because I had worked every station.

Station One was at the entrance and often run by whoever was in the office. I made a note that we would need a dedicated clerk to guard it. What if humans attempted to retrieve glor on their own? A guard would answer to me and not give others undue influence. I flicked the safety levers in Station One and walked down the line, following divots and turns like they were part of my zarata. I didn't need the runner lights. I could run around this place with my eyes closed.

At Station Two, I readied the conveyor belt to bring in glor to be cracked. Station Two was traditionally served by women because of their physiological tolerances. The initial separation of glor from other materials was more of an art than a science and was best done by skillful hand. Like I said, I've sat and worked every station, but I am not physically adept as the female Xavians at cracking glor. It's pretty hot to handle, and women have higher internal temperatures and so can tolerate the job a lot better than men. I felt powerful cracking glor, but I never managed a good job of it. It was important to understand the entire process, even if I was specialized for one part—seeking or glor-minding. The initial search for minerals had a somewhat addicting ratio of luck, art, and science. Perhaps one day our science would fully catch up and my crude nose will be replaced. Until then, I stepped into a side channel and sniffed the air for hints of the next potential treasure-hold of glor.

Chapter Twenty-Two
Best Friend

Cassie

"Dude, what happened?" Layla asked with a half-smile, appearing on the settit.

I hid my face in my hands.

"Well, that was fast." My new friend was impressed. She was about to be even more impressed when I told her about the dicks. Of course I would tell her what it looked like, but I had to work myself up to it.

I had sneaked a look when he pulled out of me and corralled them into his pants. If they hadn't made all the metaphorical stars align in my vulva and supernova, I would have been more wary of the intricate appendage.

"Does he look human?" Then she wondered out loud, "Do human dicks even look human?"

I laughed. She had a point. With a sheepish smile, I held up three fingers.

"Wait, are you serious? You need to use words for this."

"I don't even know what words to use. There's three of different lengths, and the two smaller ones can wrap around the big one."

"That sounds…complicated."

"It wasn't bad… Really nice actually. They move like elephant trunks, I guess."

"I don't know. That sounds kind of creepy." I thought she would change the subject, but her curiosity got the better of her. "How big is it?"

"Big. Like eight inches, and its thick when all three are together. I didn't climb that mountain."

"Wow, maybe I'll have to give Moto a chance," she giggled.

"At least his tongues. There's three of them too, you know."

While I hadn't sorted out all my thoughts and feelings regarding sex with Zade, I was glad that it was out of the way and Layla hadn't judged me for it. She was already a good friend. I needed one.

I couldn't tell her about the shit he'd pulled, pretending I'd be in trouble with Davian. I wasn't ready to talk about what he had against me. And I'd used him too, sleeping with him. Maybe these were red flags for another bad relationship, or maybe the score was even and we could move on.

I was ready to move on from my past lives. If Zade was in this program to have a partner and a child, I'd show him how good a partner I could be.

Chapter Twenty-Three
Food for Cassie

Zade

"Are you hungry?" I poked my head in as soon as the settit call ended. I hadn't wanted to give her a chance to rummage through the desk.

She jumped at my immediate entrance. She probably thought she was going to get away with something. Her face puffed up like she was going to be mad at me (again), but then it sank as she processed what I had asked her. "Yes, I'm very hungry," Cassie admitted.

I gestured for her to follow me to the main living space and kitchen. I pulled a stool out for her and helped her climb on top. I provided the tray of vegetables.

"Thanks. Do you have any meat or fish? Ooh, fish," she said around the green crisp she likened to snap peas.

I set to work heating the oil to gently sauté some fish. Our community eats meat and fish but not every day, and certainly not featured in every meal. The vegetables make a delightful snapping noise between her teeth. With something to occupy her mouth, she could be pleasant company.

"I don't cook a lot or eat fresh vegetables."

"I'm sorry to hear that."

"I mean, I could cook and eat fresh vegetables. It's just not always the easiest or the tastiest, so I don't."

"What do you eat on Earth then?" It took effort to farm and cook, but we didn't have alternatives.

"We have a lot of restaurants that prepare food for you. And some food we buy already cooked and then heat it up. It's called frozen food. And you can even have other people deliver food to you. That's their job."

Their system had many choices. Perhaps a population based on currency rather than agriculture had the ability to do that. Imagine that, animal meat for every meal. It sounded fairly inefficient to me, but I liked the idea of not-cooking. "I confess I don't typically cook individual meals. Usually, I cook a large amount of food and eat from it for each meal."

"So you're doing this for me?" she asked, a green crisp hung from her pretty mouth.

I tried out the shrug she often gives me. It must have been passable.

"My fourth favorite boyfriend—we told his parents he was my tutor. Anyway, his family was Persian and his mom was a wonderful cook. She'd bring down these wonderful kebabs to the basement."

"What's the basement?"

"Excuse me, I'm telling you about *kebabs*—skewers with seasoned meat on them…so good. Basements are the bottom part of a house, underground where they built the foundation."

"Tell me about the superior three."

She gave me a questioning look.

"The other favorite boyfriends. Did any of them cook?"

"Oh no. God no. My second least favorite boyfriend managed to catch the microwave on fire twice. I threw it away and we just ate cold food for the rest of the relationship." She grumbled something about several months as she coughed. A fourth favorite boyfriend and a second least favorite boyfriend meant six boyfriends.

"How many boyfriends have you had?" I asked, holding up my fingers which were slick with the wet fish I was preparing for her meal.

"None of your business," she rapidly responded.

"Why would you describe them in relation to each other if you don't want them known? Maybe *you* shouldn't be telling me your business." I knew I wouldn't get an answer quickly. I'd figure it out though…to fully understand my enemy. I wasn't getting to know her for my benefit. She was a spy, and her reports could ruin me and Xavia's future. At least that's what I told myself.

Her cheeks bunched up around her nose along with her upper lip as she thought about it. I enjoyed challenging her. I was learning her. Playing amateur against her espionage skills could be dangerous, but it was fun.

"Fair enough," she said, surprising me. She didn't often agree with me. "I do invite the question with my quantitative ranking system, but it is also purposefully vague and non-identifiable. My third favorite boyfriend could be my third least favorite boyfriend. And of course, girlfriends are on an entirely different scale."

The fish sizzled in the pan with a satisfying crackle. I grabbed an old tin, pinched it open and sprinkled the seasoning on. The spice in it picked up into the air and smoked a bit. Tiny specks of grease dotted the back wall, but it was too hot to reach back there to clean it now. It would be forgotten by dinner's end.

"Do Xavians also get their own scale?"

"I don't know. What's a Xavian mate like?"

"We don't have nearly as many," I started before dodging her least favorite vegetable flying through the air. It bounced off the fish and against the backsplash. I'd have to remember to clean it.

"What was that for?" I asked, guarding the fish from future attacks with a cooking utensil.

"The relationships I've had and how many—"

"We usually only have one."

"Oh, wow. Like penguins?"

"Who are penguins?" I was confused.

"Sorry. Please go on." She motioned with a carrot, and I flipped the fish. Probably a little late, but now it had a beautiful brown top. If only I had managed to cook the interior too, I might impress her (and me) yet.

"Rotha. Um…fate mates? I do not know the translation. Once you are an adult, you may physiologically bind to someone to become a parent with them."

"Physio…what? I don't get it. Like sex?"

A small word from a small mouth. I adjusted in my pants. "Well, sex is often involved."

"Or more like romance?" Her eyes were big. Having eaten her favorite vegetables within reach, her elbows were propped on the counter, her chin resting in her hands.

"It's not just sex or children. Rotha signals optimal reproduction and compatibility. It can physically manifest, like with pigmentation or hair changes. They're marks of companionship."

"Oh, that isn't matching make-up on your parents' cheeks?" The stool was not designed for Cassie's height. It nearly toppled over as she leaped from it.

She pulled a photograph from the living room shelf and examined the family it contained. I had dusted it, but grime had built into the corner crevices of the frame. Curved stripes crossed my parents' cheeks and jaw lines. "You don't have any," she remarked at past-me and current-me.

"Right, those are their rotha marks. I've never shown signs. Rotha isn't required for reproduction though. It just makes it more likely."

Cassie's face went sullen. The photo of the happy family was returned to its spot in the living room. Was she hoping to get pregnant and have a family? Would she do it with me? This had been Vance's dumb idea—trade glor for women, but here she was, and we'd already had sex.

"You've traveled so far. It was a large sacrifice, for what reason?"

"To meet you, to eat Xavian food, to learn about you, your language, how you live."

"Me?"

"Well, not you personally…your people, but yes, I'm learning about you."

I had the space and I could tolerate a roommate. This home had been built for more than a single guy who lived in the mines…but Cassie had become a lot of trouble. I adjusted my pants again as I moved the plates to serve the fish. If I had known that they would make human housemates this gorgeous and this hungry, I would have tried harder to get out of it. I'd ignored my Xavian duty and would have protected my privacy.

And at the same time, the place had never been cleaner or smelled as nice since I was a kid. It was nice to have more to keep him company than his laundry and his parents' old trinkets and rock collections. Literal rocks.

I refilled Cassie's plate with vegetables and the larger portion of the fish.

"I don't always eat like this," she said as she cut into fish and let the steam escape. She corralled some round vegetables all on her fork and shoveled them in her mouth. "I'm just really hungry."

"Maybe it's the space travel," I offered. Hunger was a need, and if anything, I think her shipmates needed to be hungry more often. She'd also need more food to grow a little one inside her.

Chapter Twenty-Four
Investigation

Cassie

If it wasn't for the threat of the Orkain, I would have left this cave out of boredom a long time ago. Instead, I flopped around the living space, looking through everything.

There were a lot of rocks.

It was cute. Zade's father was like one of those penguins who gift their mate pebbles for their nest. Humans traded in rocks too…diamond rings and holmium metals. But their bonds weren't necessarily for life.

What if I built a life with Zade and his real, genuine rotha mate showed up? He'd throw me, the counterfeit import, to the curb. I didn't even look like the other human women, wouldn't be worth keeping, I worried. Still, I wanted to try Zade out. Maybe we'd be unexpectedly good partners.

And what else was there to do?

Oh, cleaning. I cleaned a lot too. There was a lot of dirt. It was a cave after all. I wondered if the women of Zade's family should have been credited with expansion of the home. Cleaning and snooping went hand-in-hand. Honestly, I'd do it even if my dad hadn't tasked me. I was a nosey bitch.

I was so interested in how they lived. Obviously, because I might be continuing the tradition. I patted my tummy which I had avoided at first, afraid I'd slip up and do it in front of Zade. But I'd decided the baby needed love, and I needed the love too.

The signature creak of the exterior door sent my heart into overdrive. It was an exciting nervousness I preferred to the loneliness. Inside, I felt a flutter that wasn't mine. Wow, both of us were feeling it for this guy. Stockholm syndrome must be legit. Either way, I nearly jumped from the couch to meet him in the living room.

It always interested me in what condition Zade would arrive. Sometimes he was as tidy as when he left, and other days he was in immediate need of a shower, covered in dirt and grit. I preferred the latter, and today was one of those days. I ran to the door and he didn't turn me away.

As he'd probably done when he was a child in this house, he took off his boots and dirty outer clothes in the entryway. In the same home, it was habit. With only a pair of shorts on, he bent down to pick up his discarded clothing. I worshiped his…miner's tan? It reminded me of a farmer's tan but with dirt where his skin had been exposed. If my lip got caught up in my teeth as I admired…that was me, not the baby.

He noticed me, but his species wasn't modest. Or at least he and I weren't. That's how I'd gotten in the habit of watching. He didn't hide behind the handful of clothes either…not that I think he would succeed at hiding much.

I stared at Zade's chiseled chest and slender abdominals. Did we have all those muscles? Maybe it was easier to keep a slim, sexy physique as a Xavian. Maybe all Xavians had prominent obliques… I wasn't going to take them for granted though. I wanted to run my hands along every single ripple of muscle to remind myself they were real.

"Why are you dirty?" I asked, following him to the bathing room which was set up differently since it was in a cave. There wasn't an enclosed shower. In the center of the room was the shower head which came down from the ceiling. The toilet was separate in an isolated corner. In the opposite corner was a deep natural tub in the corner of the room which appeared to be filled by a natural source. The water remained at a set level but continuously moved.

With a few switches on the wall, the giant rectangular shower head began to spray, and steam crept across the cold floor to tickle our feet.

"Sometimes you've got to dig to know what you've got." He didn't make any gesture for me to leave. "I run the entirety of the mine, and do every job. Some are dirtier than others. *Seeking* is arguably the most important operation—finding seeds of holmium to harvest in the…" He stopped talking.

"Can't mine what you can't find," I offered.

Zade broke into a grin at that, brightening his whole face. His hair was darker with dirt and sweat and stuck to the side of his face and to his horns. I loved his devilish grin. He thought I was funny.

"So glor…holmium…is important on Earth?" His eyebrows and horns rose with curiosity. He stepped out of his underpants and tossed them aside. Christ. He was distracting.

"If that's what you are using to trade for us, then, yeah, I guess so. I was sort of hoping you could tell *me* why."

His smile faltered. "Your government referred to it as a 'rare Earth metal.' They need it for space travel."

He watched, even more puzzled, as I dragged a bench over to the water's flow and to him. My front had gotten damp, and my shirt clung to my breasts. I wasn't about to take it off though. I liked the attention on him.

I filled one hand with soap, called *soaff*, and offered him the other. He took my hand and aided me as I stood on the bench, my heart abuzz.

They don't call them knockers for nothing, but I was careful to only intentionally graze him occasionally rather than inadvertently smack into his skull.

"Is holmium…glor…common knowledge here? Does everyone know how to find it and use it?" I asked as I worked the soaff into his scalp and the roots of his lilac hair.

"No, I had to fight to keep the mine open. A lot of people don't understand its importance." He gritted his teeth as I massaged his scalp at the base of his horns. I couldn't tell if he was experiencing pain or pleasure.

With his hair slicked back, his horns were at full stroke-able height. I refrained from touching them so. Did they have feeling? Was it taboo? He didn't make mention of them, so I didn't either. I gently directed his head under the water flow, rinsing his hair. Soaff-y water dripped on his lean, hard shoulders, arms, and chest. I felt an ache between my thighs.

I stepped back. "Earth can be the same way, except there are so many of us. We can create a demand for technology and not realize how much its components are costing us."

"We didn't realize humans valued each other's lives so lowly." He worked the fallen soaff across his body. His erections indicated that he'd found our closeness arousing too.

"Yeah, that's a lot of humans—using people for personal gain." I paid less attention to the words I was saying and more to the water as it sprayed across his body.

After rinsing his arms, he arched his neck. I wanted to rake my fingers across its thickness.

"That's unfortunate. Do you do that?" The question and bluntness surprised me, but he was serious.

"Do I use others for personal gain? No, I don't… If you haven't noticed, I've gotten the short end of the stick," I said, no longer watching the sticks he was sporting. And feeling defensive.

"I don't know what that means. The stick?"

I crossed my arms over my chest. "It's a figure of speech. I was trafficked here. Usually victims of trafficking don't have a lot of chance for personal gain beyond what's allowed by their captors." Now I wasn't sure why I was feeling so hot under the collar, and it was uncomfortable. At the same time, I wondered how much a human woman went for in glor-terms.

"We are not your captors," Zade reminded me.

"I don't see any choices for me. Are you going to keep trading with Earth?"

"We continue to mine. The prince is shortsighted. I only expect a rash decision. He may decide not to deal with Earth in any capacity."

"That's noble. They don't deserve glor if that's how they treat people."

"But 'they' are also you. Doesn't Earth need it?"

"I hope not at this price," I said softly.

"Is it so bad here?" Zade had begun to win me over again.

"It depends on our captors," I mumbled, vulnerable even though I wasn't the one naked. I was ready for this to be over. "You're done. You're clean enough." I announced, resting my hand on his shoulder to help myself down.

"I will tell you when I'm done." His large hand enveloped my forearm.

My heart skipped a beat. He only turned and helped me off the bench. And with that, he'd taken back control. I preferred it that way. I trusted others' decisions over my own. At the wall, I turned off the water.

"Turn on the dryer, at least?" He pointed to the button on the far right. I pushed it. Instead of water from the top, warm air blew. Zade moved around to dry himself.

I was impressed. "Whoa, that's pretty cool. What do you call that?"

"It's warm. It's called a shower," he said patiently.

"No, this drying part."

"Your translation would be…dryer."

Well, yeah, I guessed he was right. "All your showers have a dryer?"

"Yours don't?"

"No, we just use towels."

"For your whole body? That must create a lot of laundry." He shook out his hair with his fingers. I wanted to be doing that, so I stepped into the center of the room. The air was warm but not harshly so. I giggled as my clothes fluttered around me, tickling me. I stood on the bench nearer the room's center and used my height to run my hands through Zade's thick, wet strands, dark with moisture. I finger-combed through, brushing my fingers along his horns.

"So what is it that your captors won't allow?" he asked. The words were harsh, but the delivery was kind.

"Will you show me the mines?"

Chapter Twenty-Five
Her Request

Zade

Fryyre. Of all the places in Xavia, that's where I'd like to take her least.

"Why the mines?" I asked, already tired of whatever argument this was.

"It's not that I really want to go to the mines. I'm sure your work is boring, but I can't stay holed up in this cave. I want to go out somewhere. And…honestly, that seems to be the only other place you go."

"And it's not because humans want glor?" I tried. I watched to examine her response.

Her hands fell in some sort of despair for not the first time tonight. "I don't even know what glor looks like. And I wanted you to show me, because it seems important to know about. I don't know why you think I'm such a threat."

She was so good at pushing this back at me. I had to remain steadfast, despite all that I was feeling. And I would be feeling pretty guilty if this woman wasn't a spy…was my guest…and even possibly my rotha mate.

"You don't know unless you dig," I said. I hoped it sounded cryptic and not stupid in English.

It worked. She was agitated.

"Well, I don't like you digging into me. I hate being here by myself," she said in pointed words that she threw like daggers.

I had her teetering, angry, unbalanced—right where I liked her. I stepped into her.

"It's dangerous," I chided her like a child—a child about to be given their way. My own excitement betrayed my decision.

"I promise I won't get in the way," she pleaded like a careless kid.

I did it against my better judgement, but no one else seemed concerned. I did it because I wanted to see that smile bloom on her face.

"Fine. I will take you for part of the day tomorrow, *if it's clear.*" I stressed. I could always fib about the report until I came back to my senses.

"Thank you! Thank you!" she whooped.

And in her excitement, I realized how lonely and bored she must be. Guilt ripped through my insides. I hadn't meant for her to feel trapped. I had to work and didn't want her there to learn about the glor. I gave her the entirety of the home while I was gone, having taken anything sensitive out of the house. I was at work a lot. I had to be.

#

I stretched against the tightness in my back but it wouldn't relax. I wasn't sure if it was from the sexual tension or my mounting work stress. Yesterday's conversation had gotten out of my control, and now I was late to work because I was waiting for Cassie to wake up. Impatient.

To distract myself from rudely waking her, I prepared her an early meal she called breakfast. Cassie had taught me several human customs, all of them surrounding food and meals.

I didn't often feel hungry for Xavians' first meal which was midday. It didn't matter as there wasn't anyone to remind me to eat. In the mines, I was quick to forget the time. While I wasn't hungry, I enjoyed the routine and procedure of cooking in the morning…surprisingly much more enjoyable when one wasn't already hungry in the evening and late to starting the whole process.

This morning, I cooked eggs, vegetables, and, because I felt bad, a meat. I didn't know if all humans were like this, I'd have to ask another Xavian host, but Cassie enjoyed at least one animal protein at every meal. Perhaps she had different metabolism needs. No matter. I was happy to feed and energize that beautiful body.

I plated the food on an oven-warmed dish and delivered it to Cassie's room. She hadn't woken yet, but nobody could wait for that. If she wanted to go with me to the mines, then she couldn't sleep through the day. I couldn't be certain Vance wouldn't spot my absence and create more difficulties.

I set the tray of food down loudly on the table closest to her sleeping head. Cassie murmured as she shifted in the bed. Her sleepy eyes peeked from behind her yellow hair, which she called blond. It reminded me of shiny gold, and her skin white like glistening salt.

Human furniture looked odd in my parents' room. The cavern walls had so much more character than anything you might put within them. Soft and brittle materials like wood and glass felt temporary to the slate walls my father's father had carefully measured and cut. He worked with the natural formations without undermining it. That was the trouble with homes being built underground to hide from the Orkain. They tried to recreate free standing structure and put them underground. I worried about the structural soundness and longevity. Time was a limiting factor, but more thought should have been put into creating homes from what was there, rather than burying Xavian things that didn't quite serve.

Still, with all my creativity, I hadn't considered such a damn beautiful, curvy, and soft woman existing in my parents' bedroom. Maybe if I had her again, this time drew it out and pleased her, I could stop thinking about her, stop trying to touch her.

"Ooh, what's for breakfast?" She rubbed her pretty eyes.

I pointed to things she might not recognize and told her their names. She was trying to learn a lot of Xavian vocabulary…if I hadn't learned as much English as I had, I think we still would have gotten to this level of communication pretty quickly. She had a fiery personality and was constantly talking. It was easy to get frustrated in our efforts to communicate at the speed and clarity we wished.

"I like hot breakfast, thank you, but I hope you have another reason for waking me."

"I do. I'm taking you to the mines."

Spy or no spy, her entire face brightened with her smile. I felt a twinge in my chest, unsure if I was making the correct decision. I shouldn't leave her unattended in the house anyway. She'd be liable to walk off and try to get her information elsewhere. No, Cassie was my problem.

Chapter Twenty-Six
Visiting the Mine

Cassie

Rather than a thick door fitted into a shallow cave like his home, the mine's entrance was a wide, gaping scoop out of a cliff. He waited for me to enter, but I hung back, enjoying the uneven warmth of sunlight on my face. I wasn't anxious to return underground.

"Not everyone works *and* lives in a cave. You're just lucky, right?" I asked.

"Lucky," he repeated.

Half the time I didn't know if he understood our interactions, the other half I didn't understand. I was probably teaching him poor English.

I took a deep breath, whispered goodbye to the sunshine, and stepped into the hangar-like mouth of the dark brown cliff. If its mouth shut, there would be a mountain's worth of dirt between my head and the sun. Was that a normal thing to think about? Perhaps it was the sharp smells, the darkness around the corner, or the narrow, never-ending tunnels, but I didn't much like the mines. I remembered running through them, scared, when I arrived.

My eyes adjusted to a figure approaching us. I hadn't seen another Xavian in person since we'd landed. This one was as tall as Zade, and bulkier. A giant smile encompassed his rectangular face which was topped with nearly horizontal horns. He was a darker green than Zade, and I wondered how much of that was genetic variation or if he received more sunlight than Zade. Being pale-skinned, I was saving my precious sunscreen which I had stashed in my go-bag.

"Haellea," I said, bowing my head. Had Moto done that for me?

"Haellea!" he replicated the awkward bow of my head.

Realizing my mistake, I ducked my head which only encouraged the alien's head nodding. He checked with Zade. To my horror, Zade bowed his head too. If this became custom on Xavia, it would be my fault. I pointed to myself and tried to recover. "My name is Cassie."

Zade translated for me. The man was Bern, Zade's foreman in the mines.

"Haellea, Bern," I said.

I didn't think his smile could get any bigger, but it did. He spoke excitedly to me, pointing out many things overhead and at the station. I imagined he was identifying elements and listing his duties, however Zade was much less verbose in his explanations. "He's in charge when I am not, working this station and the control board in the office."

Bern gave another little bow of his head. God, I should probably stop him, but I didn't know how without making a scene. Right now, I was the only one embarrassed. I didn't want to make it more awkward.

"Will you show me the office?"

"No," said Zade without even bothering to translate the question for Bern.

Bern followed and continued chatting despite Zade's sluggish translations. Bern was more than happy to talk to me. He had said more words to me in the last hour than Zade had said to me in all the time we had known each other. Perhaps Bern could learn English quickly too, and I could learn more Xavian. Zade appeared annoyed, but I enjoyed Bern's enthusiasm over everything.

"Bern, do you have a family?" I asked through Zade.

Zade frowned before translating.

"No, he does not. He lives with other bachelors… Why would you ask that?" Zade said.

"I'm just making conversation."

"I don't know what that means. Why do you need to know about his family?"

Another frustrating communication moment. Was there a language barrier, or was Zade being an asshole? I explained, "I want to learn more about Bern."

Bern had heard his name in the conversation, but Zade didn't acknowledge him. He was looking directly at me. "You don't need to know *anything* about Bern," replied Zade.

My guess was asshole.

"I don't *need* to know, but I would like to know." It was like arguing semantics with a toddler. "Where do they live? Is it a cavern like yours?"

He gave me another annoyed look, but surprisingly asked the question of Bern.

"They live in an underground house, but not part of the cavern system."

Zade acquiesced to more questions. Bern seemed satisfied Zade had returned to translation duties, but I remained on guard. I was highly conscious that everything was passing through Zade, and even if he didn't outright refuse to translate, he could be altering or falsely translating.

Zade tried to move me farther into the mine.

"It's hot in here." I was expecting it to be the temperature of Zade's house, cooler than the warm outside.

"We've dug deep and narrowly. The heat escapes through the air faster than the ground," explained Zade.

Maybe we hadn't been in this part when we ran through before, but it was not comfortable. I would have needed protective equipment to remain at the second station for any significant amount of time. My skin felt hot. Was the Xavian's tolerance of higher temperatures why my dad and the government were interested in keeping their population alive? Maybe they needed the Xavians to get the metal from the ground.

When we exited the mine, I'd learned a lot more about the glor process despite Zade trying to keep it from me. I was desperate to know about the material that I was traded so freely for. My life and my baby's life depended on it.

Bern reached to say goodbye or something. I wasn't sure because Zade launched between us. He said something sternly in Xavian, and Bern backed away quickly. I'd never had someone act so aggressively to protect me. I felt bad for Bern, because I don't think he meant anything by it. The intensity of Zade's anger surprised me...and exhilarated me. Zade was an overprotective asshole, but honestly, my panties were instantly wet. He could have taken me into the office and fucking claimed me there for Bern to hear—but alas, I wasn't allowed in there. So we went home. I could only hope I cooled off before we got there.

The time on the surface between the mine and Zade's home was short, but it was more than long enough for me to feel exposed and uneasy. The Orkain had destroyed nearly an entire populace, and I was new meat. The only thing that had my heart pumping more was the soft assists of a man that nearly bit the head off another for *considering* to touch me. Holmium knowledge could have fallen freely from my brain. What did I care? This man could rip my father apart and not even care to eat him for breakfast because he didn't like "early meals."

Any remnants of fear lifted as soon as I was inside Zade's home. The heavy rock was no longer threatening to swallow me. Instead it was protecting me, encasing me. I felt safer than I'd been anywhere else. Now I wondered if the same desires coursed through him.

Chapter Twenty-Seven
Undoing

Zade

I barely got her inside before I let her know. "I'm returning to the mines."

Her brow furrowed. "Why? It seems like Bern has it under control." That made me angrier than it should have. She was correct, but I didn't like to hear his name from her mouth.

"There are things I need to attend to."

I didn't want her to know that I, alone, was crucial to finding new sources of glor. I also didn't want her to know what I'd told Bern: 'Touch her again and I will fucking end you.' I'd never threatened someone's life before. I didn't even know where it had come from. Bern put his paw on Cassie and I saw green. He backed off quickly and then laughed it off. I hadn't said anything after that—didn't need to say anything more.

I had remained dangerously angry escorting Cassie for the rest of her tour. Bern had been his stupid self, talking too much and falling all over himself to please her. If they spoke the same language, Cassie would be able to extract any information enthusiastically from him. I didn't want them talking, shaking hands, or sharing whatever that stupid bow thing was. Still, was I possessive about glor information or of Cassie?

"Was it Bern? Because he touched me?"

There was his name in her mouth again. She remembered they'd touched. I bristled in anger, but Cassie didn't hesitate. She pulled close to me, playful. She was teasing me. Riling me up when I needed to cool down. Being in close confines with her, watching her, trying to protect the glor, remembering what her body felt like under me… It was a lot. Under stress, I buried myself in work, which drove what success I'd had in the mines. I'd sort of forgotten what it was like to care for something…someone else. She could be so difficult, but my life had never been this interesting before either. I secretly liked it. But everything I enjoyed could be a ploy. I had to get keep her away from Bern and the mines, and now I needed distance from her myself.

I made it to the entry for my exit, but Cassie closed the distance.

"Because it's hot that you're jealous like that. You remember *hot*, right?"

Sexy, attractive. Like her. Fryyre, she was flirting with me. I needed to return to the mines and get away from her big, innocent eyes, smoky voice, and the woodsy sweet scent of her arousal.

I stared down stupidly at her, doing nothing to stop her as her face rose to meet mine. My anger turned to passion on her lips. Her kiss upended all my thoughts. I didn't have the strength to withstand the attention she gave me.

I pressed my tongues across her lips, asking for entrance like I wanted to enter that hot little cunt. Her mouth was small and fiery. I took a quick tour, my hands along her curves, her roundness, the bulge of her breasts, curvy belly, and strong thighs. I nestled my forearms against the sides of her glorious, perfect breasts.

I wanted to smother all of her in kisses. She was a distraction. An effective diversion, perfect for me. I'd been nothing but troubled since Cassie's arrival. My cocks shifted in my pants. Cassie's arms pulled on my neck and, with it, my will. I was breaking and I couldn't stop it, falling into a deep dark hole of my own undoing. Her hands were at my pants.

I observed the way she loosened the laces and belts of my pants. She knew her way around them much better than Xavian women. I hadn't seen such laces on Earthling space regalia either. I pulled my mouth from hers.

"You've undone a lot of men's pants?" I felt possessive of her. No doubt. If it was rotha that drew me to her, putting a baby inside her would calm it.

She giggled. "Men's pants aren't this complicated where I come from. I've undone a lot of ladies' clothes."

She was kissing me again before I could ask if she meant her own clothes or the clothes of other women and for what purposes. She pressed her tongue into my mouth now as she became more urgent with her hands. As soon as my pants were loosened, I thought she would shove her hand or maybe both down there. I was crumbling under her touch, but maybe I could still break her first.

"Be patient, girl. If that's what you want, I will happily oblige, but first I'm going to taste your body."

"*Be patient, girl?*" she bristled. Her spine tensed as she considered me and readied her reaction.

"When you are impatient like a child, I will address you as so."

Different emotions flashed across her face. This was working. I'd either thrown ice water on the whole interaction or turned it in my favor.

She bit her lip and acquiesced. Her body relaxed. "Okay, daddy," she said.

I didn't know the term, but the sharpness in her tone was gone. She was submissive, obedient. Mine. I loved any words coming from that sultry mouth. The next words I would learn would be her words of pleasure. I would stay in control of this. If the only place she was willing to relinquish that power was where it came to sex, well, we had to start somewhere. And I had been hungry to taste her.

Chapter Twenty-Eight
Tell Me

Cassie

Damn. Zade was putting me in my place and that turned me on. Breathing hot onto my skin, he flicked his tongues against my collarbone. I melted like butter, oozing under his lips and along the edges of his tongues. I abandoned my hard work on his pants and instead held tight to his skinny obliques. I stopped fighting for control and trying to speed to the end.

He kissed me deeply before his tongues retreated, trailing peppery kisses along my cheeks, jaw, and ear before sucking the side of my neck. I let myself be kissed; I let him explore me while my mind wandered, love drunk. The hair on his chin tickled. A shiver and a giggle escaped me. He nipped me with his teeth, stopping my laughter mid-exhale.

No giggles, got it.

I was restless and anxious for him to move to my breasts, but he lingered on my collarbone and between. I reached playfully for a horn and pushed him lower.

"Don't do that," he warned. There was no anger.

I decided to test his boundaries. "What are you going to do about it? Spank me?"

"How do I spank you?"

Oh god. We were communicating so well, I forgot there were words he didn't know. I guessed they hadn't gone over the word 'spank' in any of his language videos. I slapped my ass. His eyes lit up at the bounce of my butt and the noise of smacking flesh.

"It's a punishment for being naughty."

"Does it hurt you?" He scanned down my body with this new knowledge. He liked spanking. I could tell.

"If it didn't hurt a little, I wouldn't learn my lesson, right? Maybe you should teach me to behave myself," I joked.

"You do need more patience," he said without hesitation.

"Hey, now—" it was my turn to warn him. I shook my head, disbelieving. Also, I needed him to continue. "I want your tongues on my breasts, please," I requested.

My politeness did not mask my impatience. My inhale caught in my throat as his hand came down on my ass in a hard spank.

"Patience," I squeaked. Oh, that stung. Perhaps he had learned a bit too quickly.

He pulled the neck of my shirt to one side and down my shoulder and kissed the fat of my arm. I wouldn't call it muscle because I don't think I could find one in there. Finally, I felt his breath along my cleavage, then his lips on my breasts, grabbing a mouthful. My tits were so sensitive, partially from horniness and partially from the coarse fabric against them. It was a relief when he removed my shirt and kissed them freely.

A small noise escaped my lips when he dove between my breasts. I loved the softness of his tongues and the hardness of his horns. He was the perfect balance of pleasure and roughness. I needed him. I wondered what it would be like to pin him by his horns and ride his face.

He put one of my breasts into his mouth and sucked. My lower half jerked, seeking friction. A heavy hand restrained me even as his heated sucking continued. My back arched. When he released my nipple, it was a swollen deep pink peak. He moved to the other breast, grazing my flesh with his teeth. I sucked in air and cried as he wrapped his lips and tongues around my nipple, flicking it and wringing it. I whimpered but did not interrupt.

I almost stopped him from kissing my stomach, but he'd kissed everything else so far. Usually my belly fat was enough to make me feel self-conscious and out of the moment. Now with the pregnancy, it felt too intimate. I was worried the baby growing inside me might make its presence known. I'd promised to behave, but the baby hadn't. I tolerated it but didn't play that it was pleasurable to me. He eventually moved from my tight, stressed stomach, downhill to kiss much closer to where I needed his touch.

He pulled the loose pants over my hips and down to my ankles. "Teach me about your body, Cassie. Tell me what I'm doing and what it feels like. Tell me what you like."

"Okay," I said nervously. I felt on display.

"That's not how you address me. What did I ask you to do?"

His smoky commands pulled me from my thoughts and I played along. "Okay, Daddy. I'll describe what you're doing and how it feels. I'll ask for what I want."

He seemed satisfied with that answer and gave a lick up the curvy side of my belly, grazing his teeth on me.

I decided to share with him, "You're making me wet. I want your lips on my pussy."

"In time, my sweet," he said in between mouthfuls of my thighs.

He went up one leg and down the other, skipping over my damp panties. "What am I doing now?"

I was supposed to tell him how much I like my thighs kissed. "Teasing me," I said.

It wasn't what he wanted to hear. He grabbed my forearm and spun me around then bent me over. He made a clicking noise, an alien version of *tsk, tsk.*

"Now I have to spank you."

I braced myself for my punishment. It was a single hard spank before turning me around and laying me on the couch. My ass stung underneath me but that didn't stop me from wanting another. Still, I liked him moving my body around like it belonged to him. He pulled my panties off and quietly stared at my wet, aching pussy. Once again, I felt exposed.

"Do you like my pussy?" I asked, needing his approval and touch. I could feel his breath on my cooling wetness. I was at his mercy.

"It is such a pretty pussy," he cooed. "I made it this wet?" He brushed his fingers along my slickness.

I only nodded.

"What do you taste like?" he asked. He didn't wait for my answer, nor did he sample from his fingers. Instead, he lowered his head for a long, probing lick from bottom to top of my center. I trembled.

He climbed up my body and whispered thickly into my ear. "You taste amazing. I am going to eat more."

I stiffened as he returned between my legs where there was certainly more wetness for him to taste.

"And this?" he asked, punctuating his question with his tongue on my clit.

I saw stars for a moment, inhaling sharply as I fell into a rabbit hole, but he had given me an order. I opened my eyes and tried to concentrate. "Your tongue is on my clit. It's really sensitive and it's my favorite way to cum."

He licked and I squirmed. Too much. He settled the pad of his tongue on me and waited until I stilled. Then he eased into it with undulating pressure instead.

Muscles tensed and others relaxed as I transformed beneath his touch. "Yes, that feels good. Start slowly."

He gently licked my clit. My eyes shot open as I also felt his tongue creep and slither along opposite edges of my pussy. Fuck, I forgot he had three.

"Your tongues are exploring my pussy's entrance."

A press on my clit was my reward. I relinquished any initial tightness and fell into his soft sucking. Like slipping into a hot bath, I felt pleasure and heat while his tongues lapped and explored. My head started to spin. I closed my eyes, bracing myself. I hadn't had anything like this since…God, I couldn't think.

"Your tongues are inside my pussy. Oh god—" There was no room for breath, like he'd filled up all of me.

His tongue was long and reaching, and he soon found my g-spot. He didn't need my verbal instruction to know he had hit a wonderful location. His undulating tongue hardly left me a moment to verbalize his effect on me. My feet and legs tingled as he worked me over. And after a steady build-up, I was ready. I wiggled to get more of his mouth on me, to get more pressure. He stopped me with his heavy arm and a handful of tit.

The message was loud and clear. He knew what he was doing, and I was only going to cum when he allowed it. I couldn't demand it.

I could only ask, so I did, "Please make me cum. I want to cum for you."

His emerald hand squeezed tight as he synched his tongues over my clit and g-spot. He was going to give me what I wanted, what I'd asked for.

I only had to ask.

Intense pleasures collided and exploded, sending pressurized heat traveling up my spine, neck, and jaw. My body wrenched out of my control and into his, where it belonged. My voiceless scream exited my open mouth, energy flying from all my extremities. My body was his and doing whatever he pleased. I'd never felt so good, but I'd never had so many tongues on me either. I gripped his head with my thighs, his bony horns digging into my flesh.

He eased up on the pressure and let me float downward. His tongues retracted into his mouth, his lips applying just enough touch to make me not miss him yet, as if he could read my body and fed on what I needed.

"I like kissing you like that," he said. Then a slow, gentle, serpentine lick that made my entire body shudder in an aftershock—something I'd never experienced before.

Holy fuck.

He settled gently inside me, another tongue resting on my clit. He was ready to start me up again as soon as I was ready.

"I like the way you kiss too." I lay in bliss. Could I stay here, on Xavia, and be safe? Raise a kid with this guy? I didn't know, but with Zade between my legs, I did feel good and safe…if just for tonight.

If just until my secrets met their undoing.

Chapter Twenty-Nine
Her Name

Zade

Between her legs was where I was supposed to be. I stayed there until her eyelids grew heavy. She murmured in protest, but nothing else as I took my arm from her side to wipe my chin. She curled up, and I pulled a blanket I kept folded on the urish and draped it over her naked, spent body.

I, myself, was reeling from the intensity of being trapped by her legs. I loved her taste and finding her favorite spots with my tongues. I drank as her channel clenched down. I would gladly worship at her altar every night, and in this moment, it kept me in control of our intimacy. She didn't have much argument left in her, which was unusual. I didn't know how much sleep humans needed, but I did know that Cassie spent a lot of time attempting sleep, awake, and restless. She didn't have any issues preceding the sleep I aided her with.

Cassie would be hungry when she woke. I prepared some meat that would slow cook until I returned home. Humans were a lot of trouble, and Cassie more than most. Even if I did have to send her away eventually, I couldn't help but care for her now. It wasn't an obligation but almost a physical *need* to please her, something I had never felt for anyone. Not my parents, not my colleagues or any friendships I might have. And that was before I thought I'd put a child inside her. Her belly grew rounder, plumper, hotter. I couldn't keep my hands or eyes off of it.

She was a frustrating woman. Even though she was still in bed and I was making her dinner—I felt the urge to leave. After one visit, she was catching on that my time invested was disproportionate to glor production. The mines had always been my escape. I needed them now more than ever as she was uncontrollable. Untrustworthy. Frustrating.

I was able to slip out without her protest. Even after the meal prep, I still hadn't completely softened. I felt like a hormonal youth and she my first set of tits. Stars, I loved her curves. I'd have to spank that ass again over how much power it had over me…

No matter. I completed deflated when I caught sight of who was at the mine entrance talking with Bern. That asshole Vance had some nerve to come around after shutting the place down.

"What are you doing here?" I asked. I wondered how long Bern had been entertaining him. He at least had the brains to keep him away from the office.

Long enough for Bern to quickly dismissed himself.

"On my way to see you and Cassie," Vance said, gesturing to a box of various items I didn't recognize. "One of the women sorted out items from the ship and we're returning them to their owners. These belong to Cassie, we think."

"You think?"

"Well, they belong to Cassiopeiasmith. Sara says 'Cassie' is a shortened name."

Cassiopeiasmith was a long name. I might shorten it too.

I eyed the box. I didn't want Vance calling on Cassie while I wasn't there. Plus, I wanted to do…what did Cassie call it? I wanted to snoop. "You can leave the items here and I will take them home."

"Bern says you were already here today. Why are you back?"

"To make sure things run smoothly." Or continue to run in the case of Vance coming to shut things down again. Perhaps he was here to annoy me because things were not going smoothly with his own human companion. I could only hope.

"You may not have to worry about that for long," he said, looking around the mine dismissively. He was still in support of pivoting the industry to building an underground kingdom. However, the glor had gotten him an influx of women to our world. He would be foolish to dismiss its value.

"I will make sure Cassie gets her belongings," I said, picking up the box while refusing to acknowledge the threat on my job.

I cut off the rest of the conversation by turning to take her things into the office. Vance sauntered back to his political corner and out of my mine.

The control board showed that everything was as I had left it, running smoothly. I glanced at the box. While I felt a little bad about snooping, I was desperate to learn more about her. I pulled off the box's lid. There were several supplies free, but also a blue canvas bag with a badge with English letters on it. I recognized

it from the captain's uniform during negotiations:
SMITH.

He was Captain Leonard Smith. And Vance called
her Cassiopeia…Smith. What did shared names mean?
Were they family related?

I pulled the name badge off of the green bag. We
could pretend it came off at some other point.

While the Orkain had murdered us, at least they'd
done it in a straightforward way. Humans were much
more treacherous; Captain Leonard Smith had
manipulated and trafficked humans. And now I knew
Cassie's secret. Her last name was Smith.

Chapter Thirty
Wanted

Cassie

I slipped off into pleasant sleep, but the loneliness returned when I awoke to find myself naked, under a blanket, alone. I stared at the ceiling and felt like an idiot for throwing myself on him. Now that the afterglow had faded, I was embarrassed. I still don't know what he said to Bern but the way he nearly growled at him. I'd never been good at controlling my impulses.

Well, guess what? I was still lonely. Despite those orgasms being some of the best I'd had in a long time, it had only slowed him down from returning to the mine, not stopped him. Even after flying millions of lightyears or whatever, I was matched with a workaholic just like my father. Crazy. Or maybe all Xavians were this dutiful?

At least he had given me a blanket. I found my clothes and shamefully put them back on. What was I supposed to do now? I wasn't even sure how long I'd been asleep. Would he be back soon? I was hungry, so I ventured into the kitchen.

Xavian food was mostly what I'd call snack food. It was a lot of fresh food without a lot of cooking or processing. So it was boring, but at least it was easy. I made a Xavian equivalent to a charcuterie board and sat down with a glass of fah, my favorite alien beverage which made me feel bubbly. It wasn't alcohol, and as far as I could learn from Zade, was enjoyed by Xavians of all ages and stages of life.

I'd never considered myself Susie Homemaker, but I could picture raising my child here. I'd never felt this safe on Earth. I was appreciative for the roof—or cavern ceiling—above my head and the protection it provided. It was peaceful inside. If this was my reality: being sheltered, fed, and occasionally pleasured by a sexy alien…and otherwise ignored. Maybe I could deal with that. Still, I needed him to want me here, because I'd lose any altruism from him once a loud crying tiny human popped out of me. Perhaps if he returned to dinner and a blow job, I could bank some of that goodwill for the future.

I'd finished eating and was on my second glass of fah when Zade returned home. He had a box that I recognized as US Government issued.

"What's that?" I asked, my heart in my throat.

"The other women claimed things off the ship. These are yours," he explained. He set it down and kicked off his dusty shoes. He pulled off his shirt to reveal his sexy torso of muscles, and my knees felt weak.

"Thank you." I'd quickly packed a small bag which I had carried to Zade's that first day and hadn't thought much about the rest of the ship's contents. I realized that was probably different from the other women. I hoped I wasn't too suspicious. I was always screwing up.

"I will take these things to your room after I clean up."

"May I join you?"

"What?" His mouth fell open as he processed my question.

I needed him to trust me, and maybe this was the way to do it. He'd volunteered for a sex mate. I was just going along with it, for better or worse.

"I want to return the favor," I said.

Chapter Thirty-One
Smiths

Zade

This wasn't going how I anticipated. I figured Cassie would look through her items while I washed. She'd realize she'd been caught. I was doing her a kindness by giving her time to come clean or craft a lie. Instead, she wanted to join me in the shower.

I hesitated to confront her now. The need to please her and all the excitement I felt hadn't disappeared. She was willing to give me her body. Why should I feel guilty about having sex with her now when she was the one who made the omissions?

I remained silent as she followed me to the bathing room. What was her end goal? Did she imagine a future with me? What if she found out that there wasn't much glor left? Would she leave me and return to Earth? The thought saddened me. At the same time, her fingers grazing even my arms thrilled me. If this is what she wanted, why should I stop her from playing dangerously?

And, by stars, she was more gorgeous by the day. I turned on the water, and before I could take off my pants, she was against me, on her tiptoes trying to reach my lips for a kiss and her hands were at my waist, undoing my pants.

I was instantly at attention, my length stressing the fasteners, making it difficult for her to undo them. We kissed, her passion colliding into me. Her taste was intoxicating, and I grabbed her round butt to pull her closer. Her hands kept working to undo my pants. I prepared my cock to twist around her hand and wrist when she created enough clearance. Instead, when she pulled down my pants, she slipped out of my grip and dropped to her knees.

My fucking good girl was so small and submissive from that view. The sight threatened to buckle my knees. What Cassie intended wasn't a noble sex act to satisfy rotha and have children. She wanted to please me with her mouth. I cradled her face with my hand. Considered stopping her. She nuzzled my fingers for a moment, wrapped her own around them and kissed them, but she wasn't distracted or deterred. She pushed my hand out of the way so she could grab the waistband of my shorts. She worked it over my cocks, and she gasped when they helped.

She'd never seen them up-close before. I demonstrated my flexibility and range of motion. From the main trunk, two cocks branched. Individually, they could extend, contract, gyrate, to navigate the complicated Xavian women's anatomy.

They wrapped around each other as one large, rigid structure as her hands stroked me. My cocks swelled and pulsed in her grasp.

"Does it feel good when I touch you?" she asked. Her warm fingers slid over me and along my ridges, pulling my lubricant from the heads in thick strings.

"Of course," I said as they rubbed against her.

She licked her lips before lowering her face onto my largest cock and tasting it. She sighed a sound of approval before taking more of my cock into her wet mouth.

Fuck, she felt good.

Her lips and tongue rolled over my cock. She couldn't put it all in her mouth. It was too long and too wide without changing my stiff shape. I extended longer and narrower in her mouth. She took me deep, and I learned what color she turned when she was wanting for air.

With a handful of her hair and a "good girl," I pulled her off my cock. She coughed, and greedily came back for more. With slobber and lubricant coating her cheeks and wetting her hair, I just about lost it. She was so fucking hot and I wanted to claim her.

"Take more of those cocks," I demanded. I pushed on her head.

She held back long enough to say, "Yes, Daddy."

I pulled her off my cock. "Why do you call me that? What does it mean?"

Undeterred, Cassie stroked my cocks with her hands. "In the strictest sense it means *father*, but I mean it more of a *master* sense. If I'm your good girl, then you're my daddy."

I liked being her master, but I also liked the thought of being a father—giving her my seed and having her birth my children. Could my own be growing in there? For now, I'd fill her pretty little mouth with my seed.

Happy with my new name, I directed Cassie's face back to my waiting cock. Her hands made way for her lips and her soft tongue—that single primitive digit.

She lapped at me obscenely with it. She creatively compensated with a hollowing of her cheeks as she tried to swallow me.

"Be a good girl. Oh, that's a good girl," I cooed.

She'd been a bad girl in the past, and that's how she'd gotten away with so much. Her cheeks bulged and contorted as she tried to obey her daddy.

Her daddy…

"Did you call Captain Smith Daddy?"

She immediately dropped my dicks, one of them falling out of her mouth. Cassie backed up, walking her hands backward to support her. Her eyes were wide. She wiped the spit off her lips. She glared at me. Scared. Angry.

So, it was true they were related. I had even guessed correctly. He was her father.

"It's not what you think," she spat out, protecting herself. "I got dumped here just like everyone else."

Her lies about being a victim annoyed me.

"You are *just like everyone else?* You didn't get any special treatment by being *daddy's* daughter?" I used her word against her.

"I didn't. I'm here," she said as if that was all the proof she'd need to provide.

"And which part included sucking on my cocks?" I asked angrily, putting them away. They'd gotten me into enough trouble.

Cassie didn't answer me. Didn't look at me. "Do the other women know that you are the captain's daughter?" I pressed.

"No."

"Do you think they'll be pleased to know?"

"No, but I was tricked all the same. I swear I didn't know what this was." Her voice was quiet and pleading as if she could still play submissive.

I laughed. I laughed in Cassie's face. I couldn't help it. Her face turned the same red as when she had my cocks in her mouth, but this time it wasn't as appealing.

Cassie left in a fury, like a swift afternoon storm, flashing and gone. She went to her room, and I didn't chase her. I removed my pants again and finished my shower. I had a lot to think about. I'd been an idiot, falling for her traps. She'd all but told me she was a spy. She'd been lying to me from the beginning. So why did I care what happened to her and what she thought of me?

Captain Smith never mentioned having a daughter. If Captain Smith wanted her to come as a spy, it would make sense to not even discuss her. He was a careful person. And if it was true that he didn't care about his daughter and dumped her here, then maybe it made sense that he didn't ever think about her at all and thus didn't mention her. He wasn't proud of her.

I couldn't imagine someone not being proud of a woman like Cassie, and I knew that meant that she might be my enemy. The fact that she willingly flew to a different planet made her brave. Meanwhile, I worked where my father worked, doing what he did, and I lived where he lived. I had ventured nowhere. Whether for her father or against her father, Cassie had done much, much more. Traveled and risked more. Cassie was impressive and not to be underestimated.

Chapter Thirty-Two
WTH

Cassie

I wiped my own slobber and his lubricant off my face, mixing it with my tears. Something was wrong with that man. Who stops a blow job? Not even my middle school boyfriend who told me I "wasn't going to hurt it" when I touched it like a delicately skinned cucumber *stopped* me. Maybe he thought I'd play with his cocks as I recounted my relationship with my father.

Yeah, no. I've got daddy issues, but not that bad.

What happened at the mines? There must have been something in that box for him to have figured it out. Would anyone believe me that I was innocent in the trafficking scheme? Did my dad know what position he would be putting me in? He probably thought it would force my hand to do what he wanted. I hated thinking about my relationships like a chess game, especially since I was only ever reacting, on the defensive to keep from being check-mated. But my survival on this planet hinged on it.

And I was still hiding a secret. Should I tell Zade about my pregnancy?

No, revealing it now would only put me in a more vulnerable position. What's that statistic about the most lethal time of a women's life being during pregnancy because of domestic violence? Me and my baby weren't about to be a statistic on Earth or Xavia. The longer my pregnancy was a secret, the bigger and stronger my baby could become. We both had to be strong to survive in this universe. We couldn't trust anyone.

Not my father. Not their father. And not this man, no matter if he was Xavian.

"May I bring in your things?" Zade asked from the hallway.

He must be done with his shower. "Yes," I answered. Maybe I could figure out what had damned me in that box. Not like it mattered now.

Zade had on only a set of loose-fitting pants, no shirt. He was killing me, so casual with his sexiness. He'd cleaned up, his hair dry and curling at the edges of his prominent collarbones. He set the white cardboard box at the foot of my bed.

I hadn't forgiven him for throwing that shit in my face when I'd been in such a vulnerable position, but now I felt calmer. I needed to control the damage— and, I wanted him to understand.

"I'm sorry I didn't tell you that I was Captain Smith's daughter. We don't get along, but I agreed to come to Xavia with him. I had no idea he was going to dump me and the other women here."

He crossed his arms. Any closeness we'd shared felt lost. "How did you know my name? Tell me the truth this time."

I could tell him about the video. The dumb lies had stacked up. "My dad left a video message for me when

I woke up from stasis. He was already gone. It showed me your picture, your name—" Zade looked shocked, so I added, "and several others like the prince, but I only remembered yours from the piercing."

Zade frowned, shook his head like he didn't believe me. "What else did the video say?"

"It said that they'd be back in one Earth year and that I should try to get information about Xavia to bring back to Earth."

"To be a spy?"

"I'm not a spy. I think my father just thought he could use me. I'm not even confident he will bring me back to Earth when he comes back."

"Why is that?"

"He obviously doesn't care for me if he left me here in the first place. And I'm not going to do what he said. Honestly, I like Xavians much better than I like humans right now."

I was on damage control. He chewed over my answers for a bit. I spent the time lining up my half-truths and lies. I'd prepared all of them to protect myself and my baby. My stomach clenched, preparing for a storm or for a fight. Would I be allowed to stay here? If not, where would I go?

Chapter Thirty-Three
Cross Caves

Zade

The next morning, I stepped outside before Cassie woke. What could be seen of the sky between the patches of green canopy was overcast and gray. It was raining steadily and straight down with determination to get everything thoroughly soaked. The jungle glowed brightly as the light of the sun reflected off of every wet surface. I didn't feel the wet, but I did feel the cold. It soaked through me like the rain soaked through the jungle. My mood was already dampened. The rain didn't matter.

I hated that I was right about her. She'd been lying to me from the start. And what was I doing but falling for it? I didn't trust myself around her. I didn't know what to believe. All of it was out of my control, and so I returned to where I had the most control, although even that was tenuous.

I didn't quicken my pace. There was no use. I wouldn't even change when I got to the mine. Going inward to the heat would dry me just as well as my shower at home.

I was learning Cassie's secrets, but had she figured out mine? She already didn't seem to think much of my job at the mine constantly monopolizing my time. My mother claimed my father didn't want to spend time with her, but now I know what it was like down there.

It wasn't the retrieval of glor that was the difficult part. It was the finding of it. And when you are the only one who can seek it with any reliance…then the mine is reliant on you. And instead of worrying anyone, you just work. *You* put in the work. And you control every bit of the retrieval and purification process because it's important to get every bit of glor, because who knows if we will keep up with demand. A delicate process that required the best to be constantly working.

I was the first in the mine that morning. I walked through it and into the natural cave system we had worked alongside and within. It had been raining long enough that I could hear water falling in the cave as it made its way through the topsoil and drained along stalactites. So while water had stopped dropping on me, I could still hear its activity well into the cave where I'd lost the physical coldness and my hair had dried. I clipped it back so it wouldn't fall into my eyes as I was working my way deep into the narrowing cave. As the ground could be unstable or not even there, in the case of a crevasse, the safety rule of three points of contact was paramount. Three points could be two feet and a hand, two hands and an ass cheek. While it wasn't too precarious, I kept mindful of three-points to get lost in the journey rather than all the thoughts I was trying to leave behind of Cassie.

I returned to the cross caves—an open, dry, dusty circular area and a choice to go one way or another. I'd been here the day I was told I'd be playing host to a human. It was supposed to be such an honor. I hated accepting anything from Vance. Then Cassie came and upturned my life. I had begun to trust her. Since then, I'd made no progress. I would sit here and do all that my father taught me…which was to guess. I worried that I was running out of guesses. Perhaps all the holmium was gone. Perhaps only someone as good as my father could do this. And he was gone.

That was the real problem.

I had a real fear that there was not any more readily accessible glor. And I didn't know where else to look. My father hadn't given me enough knowledge. He and his father got lucky, because the supply was so great. They had the easy guesses. I had the difficult guesses, and the stakes were much higher.

It would be one thing if Cassie was spying on a vast supply of glor and a prosperous mining operation, but if she learned the truth, it would destroy Xavia. And I couldn't risk that. I had to protect Xavia from her and from the truth.

So far, I had been right about everything. She knew my name because she had been told to gather information about us. I would be remiss in allowing her to stay and extract that information from me.

Unfortunately, the more I thought about it, the more it became my only course of action. I didn't necessarily have a problem with Cassie remaining on Xavia, but she couldn't stay in my cave.

Chapter Thirty-Four
My Girl

Cassie

When I woke up in the house alone, I didn't waste any time. He could be puttering around in the mines or he could be going to speak with Davian directly. I jumped up and went to Zade's bare office where I called Layla. I needed someone to hear my idea—and I needed a friend.

"How are things going over there?" she asked. Her dark ringlets bounced around her face on the screen.

"Not great," I managed to squeak out, suddenly having trouble restraining my emotions. "I need to tell you something."

I told Layla about how I ran from Colin to my father, who my father was, and how I ended up on Xavia.

As soon as Layla said, "Oh, girl. Your dad is an asshole," I knew she wasn't going to judge me too harshly. That was a big relief.

"Last night, Zade figured out my connection and is convinced I'm some spy. What if he convinces Davian and Prince Drex? I'm not in the military with my dad. I'm an art school dropout."

"They'll understand once they see you were a pregnant problem to be gotten rid of. …Sorry."

"It's the truth." I'd been my dad's problem for a long time.

"Why don't you tell Zade?"

My chest tightened. No, whatever Zade decided, I wanted it to be about me. If he didn't trust me, I didn't want to be here.

I shook my head. "Not yet. Meanwhile, I'm scared he's going to kick me out."

"You can stay with Moto and me."

"Do you think they'd allow that?"

She considered a moment. "No, but maybe they'd move me over there."

I'd hoped we'd be able to trade places. I had made a mess of this one. "You'd do that for me? Don't you want to stay with Moto?"

Layla's eyes sparkled conspiratorially. She steeled herself and shared, "Moto has been a good host. However, I appreciate the opportunity to meet new people and create new experiences—" The answer she'd give Davian when asked.

Still, I wanted to know the real answer. She was my friend.

"You're not into Moto?" I asked.

"No," she confessed. "I could never call him Daddy… He's more like a brother."

"I don't have any brothers," I said with a weak smile.

"They're not all they're cracked up to be. But I'll do anything you need. Maybe I can call Zade Daddy too," joked Layla.

My face must have betrayed my instant jealousy.

"Or not!"

I saw red when I imagined Zade on top of Layla. Maybe switching hosts was a bad idea. I liked Zade, but I'd lied and wrecked things here. I needed to make it right.

"I'm going to call Davian and request the switch. I don't want anyone to think I'm a spy. Moto's a farmer."

"Nothing to spy on there," laughed Layla. "I'll talk to Moto. I'll keep your secret, whatever you need, but…will you tell Moto about the baby soon after? He will help you. I know it. You will be safe here. But I imagine there needs to be some plan in place to help you when the time comes. Do you even know who delivers babies here?"

I shook my head, tears at the corners of my eyes threatening to spill over. "Thank you. I will. I promise."

Layla beamed and whispered. "Do you have any names picked out?"

I shook my head. I didn't. Was that a bad sign? I could barely think of it as a boy or as a girl. I hadn't even considered that I had to name it. I'd felt so overwhelmed, in so much denial. "Are there any names you like?" I asked, feeling a little embarrassed that I hadn't thought of such a thing. That reality was still far away. Maybe once I told a Xavian it would become more real for me.

"Is your name Cassandra?"

"Nope, Cassiopeia."

"Oh wow! That's…different," she said politely. "What about Cash if it's a boy? Cash and Cass."

My heart felt immediately full. I was grateful again for my friend for being excited about my baby and even now was giving me a different perspective. I'd been so worried about who this baby would be to everyone else—as competition to the Xavians, as a pawn for my father, as a threat to Zade—that I'd never considered what they would be to me. Layla was immediately pairing us together, Cass and Cash. I liked that. But all I could do was nod for fear that I would start crying again when I needed to talk with Davian in a few minutes.

"What about if it's a girl?" I asked to distract myself.

"I don't know. I'll have to think about it," she said with a smile. I wanted to know what my new friend would come up with. I'd ask her later if she would be my baby's godparent. Layla nodded. "Are you scared?"

"I am." That was easy to admit.

"It's going to be OK." She smiled peacefully at me, and I gave myself permission to rest my hand on my belly. If Layla could find joy in my pregnancy, then she had hope—here so far from Earth. And that gave me a little hope for my baby. This didn't have to be a horrible fate for us. I thanked her again profusely and then gathered my courage to talk to Davian and request the switch.

#

The conversation with Davian went better than I expected. I explained I'd been afraid to tell everyone of my connection to the captain. Apparently Zade had already shared his doubts about me.

Davian listened carefully, the skin around his horns and eyes crinkling with concern.

"Zade's uneasy. He has a lot on his shoulders as the only surviving glor-minder."

"Glor-minder?" I asked. Zade hadn't used that word before.

"Just like his father. Without them, we dig blindly."

No wonder Zade was stressed. He was the only person could find glor on the entire planet. My heart went out to him.

Davian continued. "Still, this doesn't seem like a good match."

While he was probably correct, my chest jerked with how much was left out of that statement. I still had a lot of feelings for Zade, but what little trust we'd built had crumbled with this name reveal. It was better if I was out of his hair. I told Davian that Layla had volunteered to switch hosts with me.

"I think a switch would be for the best," said Davian. "I'll check with Drex and coordinate it."

I felt conflicted about going outside. I'd only seen one Orkain that day and didn't see the attack. It was turning into the boogey man, though the flying terror felt more distant and less harmful than my father. Maybe if it snatched me up I'd have no more problems. Until then, I'd be shuffled from man to man. The Orkain was probably male too.

After our goodbyes, I returned to my room. Being able to pack up my things in privacy and completely was something I hadn't been afforded in my last two moves, so I took full advantage of it. Begrudgingly, I filled my boxes, lining the bottom of each with books and papers I had stolen away before Zade removed everything from the office.

I doubted I'd give them to my father, but I kept them anyway. Most of the stuff was harmless, I thought. I was trying to learn the Xavian written language with the books. It was difficult without having anyone to verify my thoughts on translation. If I stayed on Xavia, I was going to have to learn it anyway. Zade had become so protective of reading material that it felt wrong to learn, and so I was hiding my efforts. Plus, there was just nothing much else to do when Zade wasn't here. It wasn't like there was television.

Besides, I didn't have anywhere to return them without them being noticed. I couldn't leave them behind to be found. Without my explanations or apologies, they'd be confirmation of my lies—and ashamedly, proof that we were never a good match.

Chapter Thirty-Five
Switch

Zade

I couldn't risk my glor work and the future of Xavia by continuing to house Cassiopeia Smith. She stated she was scared of others' reactions, but she'd be treated respectfully among the Xavians. Fully confessing to being a spy, she'd still have a safe place to stay until her father's return, and it would be the prince's decision whether she could stay after that.

Even though my complaints were justified, somehow, I still felt like an idiot. It had taken too long for me to figure out the truth. And stars, I shouldn't have gotten mixed up with her physically. But Davian made me doubt. *She* had made me doubt.

I hated being tricked, but worse would be letting her do it again. My taste of her had been costly. Outing her would ensure that I would not return to her. I'd be too tempted to drink from her sex every night. Davian needed to know of her familial relationship so he could isolate her from confidential information. My whole body felt uncomfortable, restless. The idea of Cassie on Drex's or Vance's laps infuriated me.

The soil muddied around me, the water smelling of summer millcress. Was requesting a switch and explaining Cassie's special considerations a betrayal? Possibly, but she'd betrayed my trust from the first day. And she'd continue to do it. I had tried to be understanding, let my guard down. It had only complicated things and hurt me and my reputation. This was why I was thankful for rotha, because you could be sure of it. Trust was implied. Romance and partnership without rotha were too risky. I'd known there was a reason for her picking me out.

I wasn't special. Holmium was special.

"Haellea, Davian."

Davian's brows and horns furrowed together. "Zade, why are you in the mines?"

I felt my own brow twitch. Why did everyone think this mine so unimportant? They certainly enjoyed the benefits of what came out of it.

"I'm here for privacy. I have proof that Cassie is Captain Smith's daughter. She's admitted her name is Cassiopeia Smith."

"Yes, Cassie has conveyed this information to me."

"She has? When?"

"Fryyre, Zade, do you still believe she is a spy? She reached out to me just before you, afraid that you were going to exile her. She's requested to be moved from your house."

It felt like someone had punched me in the stomach. She'd already called him and headed me off? Oh, she was a difficult woman. How was she going to end up ahead in all of this?

"You will at least switch her to someone not privy to sensitive information, correct?"

"Of course. She's not requesting anyone *privy* anyway." He was still dismissing my accusations, but what surprised me was that she had a specific request.

"Who did she ask for?"

"Moto, who is hosting Layla."

"Moto? Why Moto?"

"What do you have against Moto? He works in agriculture, which is not an industry that the humans find pertinent." Nothing was wrong with Moto except that I thought him an idiot, a bully, and an annoyance. Also, he had a guest, which meant we'd be switching.

"Well, I don't need Layla to come here. I have—"

"What? What is your excuse now? The mines will mean nothing if we don't have a sustainable population." It was another shot at my job, my family, and my identity. I ground my teeth to keep quiet. His obvious favoritism toward Vance and Drex and his constant adoption of their lines of reasoning made every interaction with Davian a challenge. I tried to keep it out of this one, but he was being an asshole.

"The humans at least understand the value of glor…"

"And they can't begin to understand the value of people."

"Neither can you if you only value our reproductive worth."

"You are not incorrect. That's what led us to these issues with the humans in the first place. We need both glor and babies. You will have a guest. Please don't find fault with this one too."

I regretted giving this situation up to Davian. I couldn't expect him to handle it properly.

"Yes, Zroso," I fumed.

If there was any benefit to me having left for the mines to communicate with Davian, I at least had time to cool down before meeting with Cassie again. She had tricked me again. She always seemed a step ahead of me, and it would be good to get her out of my house. I didn't know what she was playing at by choosing Moto, the only Xavian I disliked more was Vance. Maybe it was only to piss me off.

There was no point in coming home to talk things over with Cassie. We had made our decisions. Tomorrow she would be Moto's problem.

I had planned to spend the night on the bed in the office, but I couldn't settle my body. It felt like the burn of indigestion, but I hadn't eaten recently. By the time I reached home, the feeling had settled. I decided to go to bed without food. Cassie was quiet in her room, either asleep or not wanting to be bothered. So I didn't.

Chapter Thirty-Six
Salty

Cassie

While I had packed up, I still hadn't lost hope that I'd be able to stay with Zade. Maybe if he saw that I was taking his concerns seriously by finding a new place to live, he'd realize I wasn't a spy.

I practiced my own diplomatic reasonings as I prepared for Zade's return. It felt like I had cotton balls in my mouth. I wanted to apologize to Zade for all of the lying. I shouldn't have bungled up our chances with quick sex and pretending this could work. It wasn't nearly enough, but I'd start by preparing him a meal. I made another charcuterie-like board but balanced the flavors better.

The olives are for the guests, my dad would say when he saw me devouring the salty foods he'd set out for entertaining. We rarely did, but it doesn't surprise me I could recall a fatherly scolding for any occasion.

Still, I'd eaten all the salty food and drank two glasses of fah before Zade made his appearance. I was beginning to think he'd stay all night in the mines. He was dusty again, which, as far as the stations he showed me, none of them would get him dirty like that. He was up to something he didn't want to show me in the mines, possibly exploring new areas. He was secretive, and he had reason to doubt me.

"I made you a meal—" I looked down at the half-eaten food on the table. I swallowed my annoyance over having to wait so long.

"Shower," he replied curtly without so much as glancing at the table.

I wished he was dominating me again. Even if it was only sexually, and temporarily, I relished giving him the reins. Because otherwise, I was pretty damn lost. Hopefully he and his cold shoulder would thaw in the shower. I poured him a glass of fah and then went to my room so that he could enjoy his living space in peace. If he wanted space, I could give him space.

It looked like my dinner peace-offering had flopped. My boxes were lined up at the bottom of my bed for another moving day. Another failure. The guilt overtook me, and I pulled out all the books and papers I'd stolen from his office and stacked them neatly on the nightstand.

After his shower, he knocked on my door, which I was quickly associating with bad news. He carried in some empty bags but was surprised to see I'd already packed and that I displayed familiar items at my bedside. To see he'd also concluded that I should leave hurt me more deeply than I anticipated.

He stood as staunchly and unmoved as the night before.

"I'm so sorry, Zade. I hate that you suspect me like this. I never should have called out your name. It was something I latched onto in the chaos. I didn't think it would lead me to live with you. It's inappropriate given my father's interest in holmium."

The spin of his eyes faltered. He didn't fully believe me, but at least he was listening.

I continued. "I kept these things to barter my return on the ship, but I don't want to help my father. Or hurt you."

He leafed through the items. "Why would your father not let you back on the ship?" he asked again.

"Why would the asshole dump me here in the first place?!" It was a fair question, but it still made me feel defensive. I didn't choose my particular circumstances. My eyes began to water and threatened to spill over. "It sucks that my story relies on how unbelievably awful my father is. I'm just trying to survive."

"We've given you no reason to believe that we mean you ill." He looked disappointed, like these were excuses that didn't make sense to him. Of course they didn't. He lived on a completely different planet. He didn't know what it was like. My situation was unstable—and I had this little one on the way. The silence was killing me. I wanted to scream "Where do we stand?" but I was too scared of the answer.

He huffed.

I needed to try. "Maybe I am sorry for more."

His eyes spun in question, distracting me for a moment.

"I'm sorry this didn't work out. If I hadn't been me, or you hadn't been you… maybe this could have been something really good."

"What does that mean?" He drew out each word in frustration. The language barrier was just one of many. The whole mess was exhausting.

"If it wasn't for the glor, we wouldn't have a reason to mistrust each other. Maybe things would have ended differently."

"It's not the glor. It's your dishonesty."

"I was scared! I'm still scared. I've told Layla and Davian. I don't want anyone to think I'm a spy—" I steeled myself with a deep breath. No more lies. "So that's why I found someplace else to live."

"Moto," he said sullenly.

He must have called Davian too. I hadn't chosen Moto to hurt Zade. I only knew so many people on the planet.

"I could stay here," I ventured. If he didn't want to lose me to Moto, he could keep me.

His arms hung limp at his sides.

"I don't know what to do, Cassie, because you are a really good liar. I wish I didn't know that about you."

Being called a liar hurt because it wasn't something that I believed myself to be. Actions spoke louder than words though. I'd been running scared and making a string of mistakes. It all stemmed from Colin and trusting my dad. And now I was stranded on Xavia where no one but maybe Layla trusted me.

I wanted to hate him for what he was pushing me into. But I couldn't. He was doing what he believed best. All of the choices I had made had led me here, and I could see where he was coming from. I had been dishonest with Zade who had let me into his house and into his bed.

"I get it. I'll leave." I laid down and turned my back to him.

He left in an angry huff.

It had been too much to ask. I was never going to convince him of anything; I would be in Moto's house with a whole new set of problems tomorrow. He had been right about one thing. I needed to be out of his house. I was a ticking time bomb. And I needed to find a safe place to survive the blast and the aftermath.

Chapter Thirty-Seven
Trade

Zade

I didn't sleep well at all. I paced late into the night. Cassie frustrated me to no end. She coordinated with Davian to leave but acted hurt like I was kicking her out. I'd been right about her the whole time. She had never been like the other women. She lied to me. She stole from me.

The attraction I felt hadn't been rotha. It had been trickery and deception. But if she was a spy, how did she benefit from this move? Was it just a desperate ploy after being found out? Had she finished her objective and was now moving on?

The papers she had weren't valuable to me or to the humans. Had she figured that out? Was she a terrible spy, or no spy at all?

Awake early, I prepared Cassie breakfast. I hadn't decided much more about her character, but there was no harm in providing her a morning meal, especially if I was wrong and upturning her life (again) for no reason.

"Thank you for the meal. Is it my last?"

She nonchalantly began snacking on it as if she was enjoying my company.

I wasn't sure what she meant. "Your last meal in my home, yes."

She was in a much more cheerful mood than yesterday.

"Will I see Layla today?"

"For a moment. We will meet in the middle of our places and trade as long as we get clear reports of no hunting Orkain. We feel due for another attack. Their last successful one was your arrival."

"And how perfect to grab two more," she said, setting down the brack with disgust.

Honestly, though, I hated that we had had sex and gotten so…involved with each other. I wouldn't do the same with Layla. With Layla, I could let her live here and I would work in the mines and there would be no trouble. I could go back to my old way of life. Well, besides the woman that would be taking Cassie's place. From my brief interactions with Layla when Cassie and she spoke on the settit, she seemed like a naïve, gentle woman, not like the brat Cassie was. I would have to remember to be gentler with her.

Would she call me Daddy too? I chuckled. It didn't give me the same thrill. That's for sure.

Cassie had only a few bags of things. I felt a sting that maybe I hadn't provided enough for her. She had so little to take to her new home. I would have to remember to ask Layla if she needed or wanted anything and do better this time at making sure she was happy, entertained, and satisfied. I couldn't abandon a woman in a cave while I worked and not expect her to get lonely or misbehave. Perhaps Layla would like to go with me to the mines.

Even after trying to confront her about the stuff, I still felt a strange desire to reassure her. But what do you say to someone you're kicking out of your home? The pain in my chest sharpened. There was nothing I could say. This is what needed to happen.

I still seethed at the idea of Cassie and Moto living in the same home, but Davian and the other Xavians were right. He was the best candidate for a smooth switch, and she would have nothing to report to the humans except about the state of our gardens and our agricultural processes—information only useful in our environment and for our population needs. Moto, and thus Cassie, would be useless to the human government.

For part of the morning, I wondered if the switch would be called off. It was perfect weather for an Orkain to be out hunting, cooler so that our body temperatures would be less disguised. The breeze had brought in thick clouds and visibility was poor. I imagined that most others would decide to stay inside today. But we would risk it. It had to be done.

We received messages that our path should be clear and met Moto and Layla in the jungle. They'd started earlier or walked fast and had gone past the rendezvous point. That created a tense moment before we recognized each other's approach. I didn't bother to greet Moto. It annoyed me that he hadn't followed instructions. Layla and Cassie rushed to hug and hold each other, talking in excited chatter.

I forgot that not all human women look like Cassie. Layla had curly brown hair and darker skin. Her body was small, skinny, and had little shape to it. The US government had hired Cassie for her extremely seductive body, I was sure. Layla had nothing on

Cassie. If Layla had been the spy, I wouldn't have gotten mixed up physically.

Moto was an idiot and got the women's luggage mixed up, and while we were sorting that out, the women were no help. The spoke to each other animatedly as if they couldn't speak with each other on the settit every day, and even later today if they so wished. Perhaps I had kept Cassie too isolated. She was from a planet with billions of people.

I can't completely blame Moto for what happened next. I was distracted too, and if there were any warning signs, I didn't notice until there was movement in the trees directly above us. I dropped all of Layla's luggage from my arms and ran to protect the women who were still standing together.

The Orkain swooped and pulled Cassie off the ground. I launched and managed to grab a hocked foot. We rolled in the air as it tried to kick me off and keep hold of Cassie. Her yellow hair flew about. I pulled myself up onto its back and dug my heels into its meaty legs. A gargled squawk flew from it when I punched its spine. However, it clung onto Cassie. I latched onto it as it flew us through tree branches, trying to dislodge me.

Cassie's terrified screams had been much like the others of those who had been taken, but they were also much longer, because I accompanied her to our fate. She fought from below, but it was pointless. My face was smashed against its feathered back as my back scraped against a tree, bark flying. The heat of pain and the wetness of blood felt odd. Unable to swing for another punch or reach Cassie, I grabbed two or three large feathers and pulled at the root. My ride jerked wildly. I tossed the ruined feathers and grabbed more, using them to pull myself up closer to its head. I would pull its face apart or gouge its eyes out if I could. I would do anything to rip this creature off of my Cassie. It was not going to end like this. I was going to save us.

We dipped low, and I heard Cassie's shout change as she hit the ground below with a thud. Immediately, the Orkain dragged me far from the ground again. And far from Cassie. I climbed upward as well, finding purchase and seeking its face.

"She's mine!" I shouted, adrenaline pumping through me. I would destroy anyone or anything that threatened to hurt her.

Another roll, and my jaw caught a branch, my head yanking back. The beast rotated deftly, and I contorted, painfully caught. It slipped out from between my heels last, then gravity took hold. More branches scratched at me, unable to stop my fall. I heard a bone crunch underneath me as my body abruptly changed direction, rolling to a stop on the ground.

I found my feet, and one ankle to be lacking. My shout was either anger or pain, I didn't know which. I was bleeding, but I couldn't manage any of that now. I needed to orient myself and find Cassie. That Orkain was surely on its way back to her—unencumbered and relatively uninjured. I was failing her.

I was dizzy and entirely unsure of where I was. I roared to clear my head, and my chest clenched as something deep inside drew my attention. Outside of the screaming pain of broken bones, of the need to be still, something inside me told me to move. It shifted in my body as I pivoted from one direction to the next, like a magnetic needle pointing to the pole. I didn't have time to process it, I ran with it, nearly dragging my right foot as I followed my body's senses. It was like searching for glor, those few times I had gotten it right and had convinced my father that I had the talent. I followed knowing somehow Cassie was at the other end of this pull.

Chapter Thirty-Eight
Shock

Cassie

As soon as I hit the ground, I instinctively curled into a ball. I was terrified I'd feel the beating of its wings and its arms pulling at me. Blood pounded in my ears, drowning out any other sound, but after a few moments, I realized I was alone. And lost.

The jungle looked the same in all directions. I had no idea where the Orkain had taken Zade or where Layla and Moto were. While I was thankful the Orkain hadn't dropped me from a high spot, it meant that it wanted me alive. It was coming back for me. I worried about Zade. It was larger than him and could fly. The Orkain had killed so many of his people. Would Zade survive?

I took stock of my body. Nothing seemed broken, but I was shaking like a leaf. Shock could kill my baby, but I couldn't think about that right now. I had to get us to safety. I had to take this opportunity to be gone. My knees felt weak and unreliable for my weight. My arms were scratched from the Orkain's claws but not deeply. I wondered why the fucker had tried to take off with me instead of smaller Layla. I could still feel where its body had been against mine. I hated it. I felt sick. *Focus*, I told myself.

I couldn't find my way back. I was completely and utterly lost, but I could at least try to put effort into making sure that the Orkain couldn't find me either. The Xavians kept to the deepest parts of the jungle and had built places underground. I needed to find cover. I looked all around me and picked a direction where the trees looked the densest.

I walked until the jungle got so thick that I scrambled on vines and became scared of how dark it had become. My cheeks were wet, and I didn't know when I had started crying or how to make it stop. I stopped to contemplate a place to be sick. Anywhere, right? I spit up and covered it with leaf litter, like an animal. I needed to pull myself together, otherwise I was going to die of panic, exposure, and shock before anyone had a chance to find me.

Stay calm. Breathe, I told myself, but at the same time, I looked for an escape. I saw a tree that had fallen on another some time ago. I moved to check out the potential hiding spot. Zade said the Orkain hunted using heat signatures. If I hid myself under these trunks, my heat should be broken up or maybe even blocked. It was dark, soggy, and I tried not to think about the bugs that were also probably calling this place home. Sodden wood and dirt sucked the heat from me, and I shivered. It was a good hiding place, but too long and it would be the death of me.

I'd taken shelter in some rotting trees, lost, and unsure if anyone would any look for me. Someone would come, right? I would take lonely and bored in Zade's cave any day to this. If not Zade, the other

Xavians? Did they send someone for that first woman? God, no. She was just gone. Would they think the same of me and Zade?

I could count on Zade. He wouldn't leave me out here alone. He'd be here soon. I'd done this all wrong. I wasn't a spy; I shouldn't have played one. I should have offered everything I'd stolen when he first confronted me. I should have thrown myself at his feet and offered to be spanked for my crimes. I'd been too stubborn, and it was one mistake on top of another. I deserved this trouble, but I hoped I could get my baby out of this mess. I held my belly and didn't stop the silent tears from falling and adding to the dampness of the decaying tree around me.

"Cassie," said Zade from seemingly nowhere, offering me his arm to pull me from the rotting vegetation. It wasn't until his heated arms were tight around me that I realized I was nearly vibrating with fear.

"Ow," I said, pulling back. Something sharp came between us, where his horn was…had been. His horn had been torn into a jagged edge. "Oh babe." Now I hurt for him.

He winced as he reached up to examine the broken horn. Fuck, that was my fault. He wouldn't have been out here if I'd made one good decision in my life. Tears ran hot on my neck, falling into my shirt, giving me goosebumps.

"The Orkain?" I asked him.

"Out here somewhere. I found you first."

I didn't know how he did that, but I was thankful.

"I have to take you to Moto's," he said.

"I don't want to go to Moto's," I said dumbly.

"I'm sorry, but you must," he said, holding me at an arm's distance. "Are you OK? Can you walk?"

I nodded and wiped the tears off my face in preparation for moving. Zade limped. His ankle was swollen up, huge next to the other. I wasn't a medical professional, but I expected it was broken. "Can *you*?" I asked. My stomach churned. He'd been running on it to get to me.

"I can get you to Moto's. It's closer."

That's why we were going to Moto's. Both his arm on my shoulders and his grimace were heavy as we made our way out of the jungle.

Chapter Thirty-Nine
Moto's

Zade

For the first time in my life, I was thankful to see Moto's childhood home, but only because it meant a shelter for Cassie. Temporary shelter. I would not trust Cassie to him. Anger seeped in as soon as he greeted us at the door. Why was he not out looking for Cassie after taking Layla to safety? Layla rushed Cassie to the bathing room and out of my presence.

Moto moved to help me inside, but I waved him off. "Call the doctor so he can check on Cassie."

Heat rose in my chest; the same sensation that had helped me find her. Was it rotha? I remained skeptical. I grew up in this jungle. I probably recognized my way. And now? It had been an intense day and adrenaline was still flowing. Of course, I wouldn't want Cassie taken from my sight. Still, I wished I'd been in any shape to take Cassie back to my home and cared for her myself.

"For you as well," he said, closing the door behind me. He left for the settit.

I wondered if they'd alerted the doctor that he'd be needed or if we were assumed gone like all the others. He'd seen that thing fly off with both of us. How many times have people not come back from that? I was just as angry with myself as I was with Moto, or the Orkain that came down on us, because Cassie had been put into this situation because of us.

Even though I was in the home of someone I didn't respect much, I stayed in the front area and gingerly took off one of my boots. I figured the compression of the other boot was helping the broken ankle, and so I left it on. I brushed the dirt off of it, which caused me to grit my teeth in pain.

I tried to clean myself up, but I had forgotten that my shirt was basically in rags on my back. At least it was a layer between my bloodiness and Moto's home. I dragged myself to the kitchen sink where I washed my hands and arms and face. There was more blood than I anticipated there as well.

"The doctor is on his way. I told Layla and Cassie. I'm going to run out and meet him halfway."

"How are they? How is she? I will go with—"

"You can't. Not on that ankle. Sit." He pulled out a kitchen chair for me. He went down the hall and came back with a pillow from his bedroom, I guessed. He set it on another chair, then approached to help me move.

I tried to wave him off. "Go!"

"The sooner you get in this chair, the sooner I will leave," he said.

Now in safety, I was growing stiffer and more uncomfortable by the second. Much to my embarrassment, Moto helped me to the chair and positioned the other for me to rest my leg on. He was much larger and more able to maneuver me than Cassie.

"Now go," I said gruffly but thought differently of him when he left. Maybe he wasn't cowardly. I was thankful as he was more able to help Cassie than I was currently.

Moto had checked on the women and said they were OK. I stayed out of their room to maintain their privacy, and honestly, I couldn't stand the thought of standing on my ankle again, but I kept an ear out for any of their conversation. I wouldn't blame them if they were mad. I had put us into this situation, for what? To hide my dead father's secrets about glor? To make sure Cassie's father lost in some galactic trade-off in which he tossed in his only daughter? None of it was worth Cassie's life. I'd been an idiot.

Chapter Forty
Rotha

Cassie

Moto opened the door a crack and spoke through it. "I am getting the doctor. Do you need anything in the meantime?"

"No. The doctor, please," Layla called out.

"I didn't land on my belly. I might be OK," I said.

"What happened?" she asked.

"It dropped me when Zade was fighting it. It flew low first. I think it was going to come back for me."

Layla shuddered. "The doctor will check you out. You'll be okay."

"Go check on Zade, please. He's really hurt." Everyone was worried about me, but my heart was with Zade in the other room.

Layla and Moto had seemed shocked to see us. Moto must not have believed we were coming back and probably told Layla as much. Isn't that what we were told about the woman on the ship? I wondered if she had been taken and where. They expected us to be dead, but Zade didn't give up on me. He believed the worst about me, wanted me out of his house—and yet he risked it all to save me. It was a shame I'd betrayed him before I knew he'd be the best thing that ever happened to me.

Layla returned with blankets to drape on my shoulders. She took a warm washcloth and washed my face.

Heljin, the doctor, was an older Xavian with a broad and soft frame. His shoulders hunched gently, and his hair was graying.

"Oh my! How long have you been pregnant?" he asked, staring at my belly before approaching me, imploringly.

It felt like a dam broke. Layla held my hand as I told him all the dates I knew, my suspicions that stasis wasn't so much a 'pause' as it was maybe a 'slow.' Heljin had a good bedside manner and listened intently.

The doctor examined me and took my vitals. I was worried about my baby and wasn't prepared for the wave of relief and joy that came when Heljin used a device to let me hear my baby's heartbeat for the first time.

"I hear you," I whispered.

The reassurance was short-lived as I doubled over with a sharp sensation, jarring the device from my belly.

"What was that?" asked Layla.

It felt like a pit in my chest. The sharpness dulling to a buzz. I didn't know what had happened, but the doctor's eyes widened with recognition.

"It's not your baby," he said to me. "Here, stand up."

He helped me off the bench and escorted me from the bathing room. I shuffled, feeling uncomfortable and wondering why he was forcing me to move. When the door opened, I felt a small wave of relief. And when we stepped into the hallway and I saw Zade, the feeling gnawing in my chest vanished. The doctor was right. It was nothing to do with the baby. It had to do with Zade.

"That's rotha," said the doctor, beaming widely. "Zade is your rotha mate."

"But she's human," said Zade. He looked at me, confused.

"What's rotha?" Layla asked.

"Rotha is the bond between optimal couples. It's a sign you and Zade should be sexually able to reproduce. That is, after you recover from the human birth."

Shit.

"The human birth?" Zade's eyes spun literal pinwheels, staring openly at my big belly. He clutched his chest.

"Um, yes."

"Can we speak in private?" he asked me, his eyes large.

I didn't realize I wouldn't have a moment to prepare myself before telling Zade. This wasn't how I was planning to do it.

"That can wait. I really need to finish my examinations," said Heljin to Zade, oblivious to the news he'd given him. "Are you experiencing rotha signs yet?"

I was surprised when Zade said yes. He knew about this and hadn't told me? I guess we both had our secrets. They were all coming out in the open now.

"The rotha pains are sharp at first, but they'll subside as your relationship develops," he explained.

Our relationship? What sort of bond was this? Did this have to do with our having sex? Add it to my list of mistakes, I guess. Layla and I gave the doctor and Zade privacy while he treated Zade's wounds. I promised to talk to Zade afterward, but Heljin gave him something for the pain which made him woozy.

"He'll need surgery on that ankle tomorrow," Heljin said, mentioning that the worst damage was sustained by applying weight to the broken bones. That was another blow to me… He'd been the only one to look for me, and did so on a broken ankle. Was that because he cared for me, or was it because this rotha-bond thing made him?

My questions remained on my tongue, because I wanted to hear the answers from Zade. And at the moment, I couldn't. But I did watch him rest fitfully on Moto's urish. Even in another room, I could feel the dull ache of missing him. What would this mean for our separation, if he was still intent on me staying with Moto? What if I returned to Earth?

I felt once again lost, without a home. It had felt like maybe Zade was my last real chance… This rotha proved my feeling had been right. Now was it too late? Would Zade accept me and my baby? I hadn't spied on him and the Xavians to become powerful or for some other selfish reason. He had to see I was just doing my best to survive. It had been a mistake.

I rested my hand over my unborn child who was somehow still with me. How many mistakes were too many?

Chapter Forty-One
Drifting

Zade

Pregnant? I felt stupid for not seeing it until now. Her body had changed in the months she'd been with me. I was too caught up in how magnificent she looked instead of thinking it curious that she was getting sexier. I didn't mind the idea of a baby growing in her belly. It made her hot… It wasn't my baby, but that didn't mean her body wasn't amazing while it created life. It was sort of a primal thought: she was fertile and I could put my own seed inside her, impregnate her, make her belly swell again.

The doctor injected numbing medication into my ankle, but it hadn't taken before he began poking, prodding, and manipulating the joint. The pain was intense, and Cassie's swollen belly and my hardening cock were quickly forgotten. I gritted my teeth. How I had been able to run on it was beyond me. It must have been rotha physically driving me toward her during my search.

Rotha did absolutely nothing to mask the pain now though.

"If it wasn't broken when you fell, it is now. You will need surgery to set the bones."

I didn't argue with him. I couldn't tolerate the pain of his examination. I'd prefer his repair be done under sedation. Anything to get him to stop touching it now.

He handed me some pills, which I swallowed without much thought. Heljin then turned his attention to my back. In the same fashion as my ankle, he sprayed a topical anesthetic but did not wait for it to set in before beginning his process of removing bark and other specimens of nature from my skin.

When he was done torturing me, he called Cassie and Layla back in. I was anxious to speak with Cassie. Why hadn't she told me about the pregnancy?

"Nothing is too deep back here. Someone can help you clean in the shower and spray you with this antiseptic. It will form a skin while yours heals. Stay off your ankle. Have someone bring you to surgery in the morning after the first sky search." The doctor said all this in English, which I understood to mean that he expected Cassie to be the one to help me in the bathing room and with my back.

According to his expert opinion, we were rotha-bound. It was my only explanation for how I was able to run directly to Cassie after I was knocked off of the Orkain. It's how I was able to get to her first. The doctor confirmed what I had already figured out hours ago. I didn't realize that Cassie could experience symptoms too. Would she accept me? Would she grow rotha marks? Or would she continue to reject me?

What about her baby's father? Did she have someone she wanted to go back to? Suddenly, all the medications set in at once. My head felt woolly and my arms like weights. I could no longer feel my foot. Or the other one.

Cassie was whisked away by Layla, which made me angry and confused. Moto and Heljin helped me to a spare room. I fought them the whole way. I had needed help fighting the Orkain, not here. I could get in the damn bed. I stumbled over my foot which felt like a club. The room was simple, spartanly decorated. It occurred to me that this would have been Cassie's room if the evening had gone differently. Maybe she'd share this bed with me, and I would have one more night with her. That would be nice.

I laid on my stomach with my knee bent. Someone brought pillows and propped up my ankle, which was nice. Someone washed my back and sprayed it. I hoped it was Cassie and not Moto, but to be honest, I was pretty out of it. It could have been Prince Drex himself.

Chapter Forty-Two
The Journal

Cassie

Heljin left us to prepare the surgery studio while Zade snored. We would wait on that talk. Layla made four glasses of fage, one of which went cold on Zade's bedside.

We drank three at the large wooden table.

"We won't switch if you are rotha mates. You'll go back home and care for Zade," explained Moto.

It's what I desired. But I couldn't discount what Zade wanted just because he was in some drug-induced sleep. It was pretty clear what he wanted. He even admitted to experiencing rotha symptoms, and he still requested I leave his home.

They said it was "rotha," but I was worried it was because of the baby growing inside me. Was Moto trying to dump me back on Zade? Did neither want me at their house?

"If that's what Zade agrees to, I will go back. But if he does not want me there, am I still allowed here?"

Layla put a reassuring hand on my back, but even she waited for an answer.

"Of course, if you need a place to stay, but if you are really rotha mates, you will not."

Maybe it meant something in his language and culture, but it felt like a nonanswer in mine.

"What about my baby?"

"Your baby too. We treasure all mothers and children. Zade will ask for you to come back. If not, he's as dumb as he thinks I am."

I didn't want to step on Moto's toes, who I might be living with. At the same time, I wanted to hear what someone else thought of Zade.

"You two have known each other for years," I led carefully.

"He always thought my family was dumb for being farmers." Moto was quick to explain. "We lived off the same land. They use their noses, which doesn't seem that different from my hard-working hands. He thinks his intelligence is a good enough reason to boss everyone around."

A chuckle escaped me. That sounded like Zade, all right. As did the rustling in the other room. I excused myself and hurried to his side. I wanted to have that conversation with him as soon as he was able and desired to have it.

I also didn't want to leave him unattended with my things. I had one item I hadn't given up. It was his father's journal, and I wasn't even sure if Zade knew it existed. I recognized enough Xavian language to know it contained personal details about Zade's family as well as information about glor mining and its chemical makeup. Davian confirmed that Zade and his father had personal abilities that helped them find the glor veins inside the caves. If that was the case, the reflections on such attempts seemed of equal importance as map layouts, especially because I'd realized from my trip to the mines that humans would struggle to maintain the mines by themselves. The Xavians tolerated the environment much better and were needed to find the glor.

Yes, if I needed off Xavia, I could buy passage for my baby and me with the journal. And then I'd find a way to stay away from Colin, because that's what I do. I run away and keep safe.

It hadn't steered me wrong yet.

Chapter Forty-Three
A Mother

Zade

I drifted off to sleep, and when I woke, I could tell it had been a long time. For one, I was a lot more clear-headed. Still on my stomach, I tested my ankle by shifting my foot. It fucking hurt, but I wanted to roll over. That's when I realized Cassie was on the bed with me. She had changed and looked like maybe she'd slept, but now was up, watching me. She helped me roll over, and I thanked her. My back felt a little tender, but it was nice to orient myself upright. My ankle screamed during repositioning then settled into a dull ache.

"Captain Smith is *your* father, right? Not the child's? You didn't lie to me about that?" I asked ruefully. I hated that that was my first question. I was tired of all the lies. I wanted to know the truth. Best to get the most painful questions out of the way.

"Yes, Captain Smith is my father. The baby's father is another human. I ran away when I found out and got on the ship with my father. I thought it was going to be a six-month vacation and we'd be back."

Running away. She did that a lot, huh? With the pregnancy, her story made a lot more sense. That's why she was collecting intel. "You wanted to trade glor info for a ride to Earth if necessary," I said.

"Yes, that's what I've been telling you!"

"You have been," I acknowledged, but now it was finally making sense. I wished she'd been more honest from the start, but maybe she had been scared. She'd been positioned by her father as my enemy, but it wasn't personal…to her. But what about the Xavians? What if her information had hurt us? Or me?

"I was scared. Will my baby be safe here?" she asked.

I didn't understand. No one was safe here. She'd almost been taken.

"I'm not talking about the Orkain. I'm talking about the Xavians. You are trying to have Xavian babies, not human ones…"

"What?! We would never—" I had trouble even finding ways to finish the sentence. Every time I thought I understood where she was coming from, I was reminded of how awful the beings were where she was from.

"OK. That's what Moto was trying to tell me."

She'd been talking to Moto? "What did Moto say?"

"Any birth is a celebration for a dying race."

That sounded a little poetic to have come from Moto, but he was correct.

"You and your little human one can stay with me," I offered softly. I couldn't stand the thought of someone else caring for her anymore.

"Because of *rotha*," she said, trying the word in her mouth. She made a sour face. "It's like your duty."

"Well, yes, but no." Her tone had taken a change, and I wasn't sure if I understood her.

"It's not because of me. You were kicking me out."

"I didn't think you could be trusted," I still didn't really know if she could be trusted. She'd now told more truth, and we were rotha-bound, but she was right. How did that change how I felt about her?

"And now with rotha, you know I can have your babies. What if I don't want to stay here?"

"Then we will do everything in our power to make sure you are allowed on the ship when it returns. We won't let them abandon you here."

Cassie seemed relieved by my answer. Knowing she had options seemed to give her peace.

"And the rotha pains?"

"They don't last forever." They'd fade with physical proximity and with time. The opposite of forever was only temporary.

She was quiet for a moment. "I would rather live with you. Maybe we can see how it goes." Even though nothing was certain, this seemed to settle her. Surprisingly, she nestled into my chest and arm. She looked beautiful there, her round body soft against mine. "Thank you for saving me."

I didn't know how rotha was going to turn out. But it felt impossible for a good relationship to be built on a foundation of lies. And, I still had mine. I'd tossed her out instead of telling the prince we have no more glor to trade. I'd rejected her because I was more interested in power over empty mines. My mind must have been empty to choose anything over Cassie. With her, I could have a new life. Without her, I was lost. I needed to tell her and everyone the truth.

Chapter Forty-Four
Surgery

Cassie

The next morning, several men arrived to transport Zade to the small hospital on the edge of the abandoned town, Frustnerrd. They used the hospital when they needed a sterile environment for surgeries. Most other cases only required house calls from the doctor or to go to the care clinic he had set up.

The hospital was not much more than a small clinic and surgery suite, but it worked for their population and didn't look much different than health care centers on Earth. It had the same sterile white tile and bright fluorescent lights. Not a fun place to be, but I was grateful that it existed. Heljin said he'd prefer I birth the baby at the hospital if possible since it was his first human birth. Mine too.

Heljin reported the surgery would be fast, a simple setting. Zade was required to rest for a few weeks, and that meant he wouldn't be going to the mines. Secretly, I was glad. It gave me a chance to spend time with Zade and for us to figure out if this was going to work.

After the surgery, we were dropped off at Zade's home. My baggage had been brought back, and Zade was still under the effects of the anesthesia and pain medication and so slipped in and out of consciousness. At least the other Xavians trusted me enough to care for Zade. I took the time to unpack when he was sleeping.

I had really blown things. He'd only taken me back because of this rotha-thing. He still didn't trust me. And he shouldn't. I still had his father's journal, and while he slept, I was learning to read it. It helped that his father spoke of the same things over and over again. Mostly the mine, but also of his wife and his son. I couldn't make out all the details, but it was evident those were the three things Zade's father cared about most, with the mine being first. Zade seemed to have adopted the same priority.

After I unpacked, I checked on him. He was sleeping. I gently laid down next to him. There was no harm to it, right?

The holmium must be important to him. It seemed important to everyone. I had to decide how important it was to me. None of it felt important now that I was against his warm body. It felt heavenly, divine. I hated that he was hurt, but I was glad that it forced him to be still instead of pushing me away or running off to the mines. How could I help him get to know me, the real me?

It had to start with honesty.

It had to start with vulnerability.

These were things that relationships were built on. Nothing that we had. And when all had seemed lost, we had been bonded together by this rotha-thing which supposedly meant we were destined to be together. It seemed impossible, and yet. Everything was backwards.

I put my arms around him and felt the baby between us, responding to our warmth. There were so many possibilities.

"I want to try us," I whispered.

Zade slept on.

Chapter Forty-Five
Waking Up

Zade

I drifted in and out, unsure what were dreams and what was not. In one, my mom cooled my head with a washcloth. In another, Cassie was lying next to me, a never-ending source of warmth. She smelled good, the soaff taking on a different life on her body. I buried my nose in her soft yellow hair and hoped I wouldn't wake up if this was the dream.

Eventually, my bladder alerted me to which reality it was present for. Surprisingly, Cassie was still by my side. And she did smell great.

"Are you sniffing me?" she giggled, not quite as asleep as I had thought she was.

"You smell good," I said honestly, still feeling a little dopey from my drugged sleep.

She smiled. "You smell *better.*"

"That might be the rotha, because I know I haven't showered recently," I said.

"I might have washed you up a bit."

That might have been that mom dream. Yikes. Hope I hadn't said anything stupid. Well, like more than usual. Speaking of. "I have got to pee."

I wasn't sure if I'd get a chance to lay back down with her, but I felt like my bladder was going to explode. I moved to get up, but Cassie grabbed a bottle from the table next to the bed.

"You're supposed to stay off your ankle," she said apologetically.

For the first time, I paid attention to my body instead of hers. My ankle was bound. I decided better of it and accepted the bottle. *This time.* I wasn't going to be held up for long.

Cassie slipped out of the room and returned with water to replace some of what I'd peed out. She also brought me food, but I wasn't ready to eat yet. Cassie wouldn't take no for an answer. She threatened to hand feed me, and so that's when I ate but only if she agreed to eat with me. She needed care too.

"When will you have your baby?" I asked.

"Three more months, I think."

She explained how she thought stasis had slowed his growth so she was uncertain how far along she was.

"The father doesn't know?"

"Colin. I didn't tell him. He doesn't know. I don't want him to know. He's not a good man."

I had yet to meet a good human man, so the fact that Cassie described him the way she did meant he was likely beyond what I could imagine.

"I didn't have anywhere else to go," she said.

She had to be desperate to get onto a rocket ship while she was pregnant.

She continued, "But I can't take advantage of you or the other Xavians. That's where I'm drawing a line."

"Drawing a line?" She didn't have any utensils or paper.

She leaned over the bed and brought up a leather journal of the kind I recognized instantly. "I choose to trust your people and you."

I thought I had them all. I did have them all. They had a lot of sensitive information about the mines. They were all accounted for, I'd thought. This one I didn't know about.

I paged through it. It had a lot of personal notes. This must be one of his personal journals and so wasn't on the inventory record. It still had a lot of sensitive information in it. "You had this?" I asked.

She nodded. "I've even translated a lot of it," she said.

That didn't surprise me. I had been certain she was trying to learn the language. What her motivation was, I hadn't known. I swallowed. Partly, I was angry again by the betrayal. She'd tricked me again. But she also could have kept it. Instead, she was returning it to me. "What did you learn?"

"Where you got your obsession with work from," she said wryly. "Your father cared about both the mines and his family, which is more than can be said about my father. He only cares about work, and sometimes family, but only as it impacts his work."

She tilted her head toward me, eyebrows rising in curiosity. "What kind of father do you think you'd be?"

The question surprised me, although I guessed it shouldn't have. She was with child. She was thinking about what she would be like as a parent, what her own parents were like. She had even formed an opinion of my father.

"I think that's why I didn't want a mate," I said more frankly than even I expected. "I'm…what did you say? Obsessed with work. That's not good material for a mate or a parent."

Cassie nodded. I didn't know if what I said had upset her or not, but I'd continue to be honest with her. She could still switch hosts. Perhaps Moto would be a better father. And then there were the billions of humans back on Earth. Moto and Cassie didn't have rotha though. We did. My parents had rotha too, but that hadn't made him a good father or a good mate to my mother. I could see that now.

I handed the journal back to Cassie. "Where are you in your translation?" I asked.

Cassie looked surprised and then settled next to me. She skipped past the drawings. I noted the dates on the pages. I had been a toddler. When she showed me the page, I knew why it had drawn her interest. She may have recognized my name and "glor" multiple times in this entry. I read through it quickly and silently before summarizing.

"It says, 'Zade came to the mines with me.'"

"How old were you?"

"A toddler, learning words," I told her for reference.

"You were so young to be in a mine!" she said, shocked. She also settled in, eager to hear more. It didn't feel like prying about glor. She wanted to know about me.

My throat dried as my thoughts flitted between trust and worry. I translated directly, unsure what the outcome would be. "Zade has the gift. Everywhere he wanted to climb, I later found a small vein of glor. He's going purely by instinct," I paused to compose myself so I could say the last part out loud, "I'm a very proud father."

"If the gift is genetic—passed from father to son, will you need a Xavian mate?"

I hadn't thought about that. "I don't know."

Tears welled in her eyes.

"Why are you sad?" I asked.

"I'm afraid you won't want me if I can't give you a glor-minding child."

She knew the term, but she wasn't worried about the glor. She was afraid I'd reject her. Maybe I could blame the drugs Heljin gave me earlier, but I couldn't tolerate her tears. Cassie shouldn't feel like this when there was no holmium to cry over. "It won't matter. My child wouldn't be old enough to help in time. I haven't been able to find new sources of holmium. We've exhausted our supply."

"What do you mean?"

"We gave your government almost all we had. We won't be able to keep up with production to keep this program alive...if it should be kept alive."

Cassie gave a little bark of laughter. "It serves my dad right."

"What does that mean?"

"It's what my dad deserves—nothing."

I didn't realize the burden I was holding would lighten with Cassie's laughter. And I was beginning to realize it was because, even without glor...I still had Cassie. What was new and possible with her seemed much more exciting than what had been lost in those mines.

My hand drifted to her voluptuous thigh, and my heart leaped when it was accepted. Maybe it was the drugs, but it felt like all the resistance we'd had between us was fading. And what was left was enthralling, electric. Don't get me wrong, this still felt like a bad idea…like falling into this would be the death of things, but *things* I didn't much care about anymore. I wanted her even as my death.

I kissed her, and she kissed me back.

Chapter Forty-Six
Ride

Cassie

Zade's touch sent fire and chills through my bones, giving me life after so much pain. I get it now. We had been pushing each other away. He had his own fears about holmium and relationships. His own history.

I kissed him gently, but the way his tongue dipped along my bottom lip edged us into *heated* very quickly. I didn't want to take advantage of a man who'd just gotten out of surgery, but his hands roamed me freely.

"Your body is amazing," he whispered.

A scoff escaped me.

"You don't think so? Another thing you're wrong about," he said simply.

I laughed. He brought me so much joy. However, he wasn't finished. He was serious. Zade put his green hand over mine and guided it over my body.

"Close your eyes and feel," he said as my fingers traced my collarbone, slid down soft skin to a prickled nipple, rode the waves of my ribcage and belly, scooping up a thick leg and ass.

I smiled to humor him. He was an alien. He didn't know what beautiful humans were supposed to look like. Although I guessed my companions were of that caliber. I wasn't though and had only gotten more pregnant.

Language barrier be damned, he read through my smile. "You don't have to be convinced in this moment. I will spend every one after this teaching you otherwise."

Zade didn't return to kissing my lips. His tongue flicked against my neck in a way that made a desperate need bloom between my legs. As he traveled along my collarbone, I saw glimpses of the perfect paradise he treasured.

He slid gingerly down the bed so that he could reach my breasts with his mouth. They were big and tender. He circled and groped them with his three tongues. It was obscenely hot. I was wetting my panties imagining those tongues dancing on my clit. Zade pulled me onto him, straddling him as his cocks nudged my back, dropping my breasts like globes of tasty treats for his mouth.

I was so wet and wanting him. I pulled my hips back to ride over the length of his cocks, but his hands stopped me. Instead, he pulled me forward, my damp panties grazing his chin.

I couldn't say I wasn't intrigued, but I hesitated. His hands grabbed ass behind me.

"I don't kn-know. I'm big," I disclaimed, thinking about how my belly would fall on his forehead, that I'd suffocate him with my thunder thighs.

"You're perfect," he said but stopped pushing on me. He cradled each ass cheek like a seat, tilted his chin, and licked the hems of my panties. Gooseflesh erupted. A fire danced in my core as his tongues walked across the thin, soaked fabric.

I lost my line of thought, my excuses, as his tongues came together in a 'come hither' motion along that apex, urging me forward. My hips took on a life of their own as they rolled over his mouth.

A fury of sensations overtook me. My hands on the cool wall. His thick wet tongue against my leg, then pushing aside my panties. Curses slipped from my mouth as his took my wanting cunt. He kept me planted on his face, handfuls of ass driving my hips down. Heat rushed through me. I couldn't hold onto the doubt when my sense of self was starting to fall apart. I melted fast, becoming one with him, getting what I needed from his sweeping tongues. With each wave of pleasure, I lost more of myself.

A strong tongue undulated deep inside my pussy; another wrote soft messages on my clit. Intense desire twisted around my spine, moving me as electrical currents shot through. I reached behind to brace myself, to relieve the weight from Zade's head. Over my shoulder, Zade's cocks were erect and reaching. He evidently enjoyed this.

He also did not tolerate my repositioning. He grabbed my wrist tightly and pulled me upright, stacked over his mouth. I peered down at his eyes, which scolded me. He knew how to order me around even with his mouth full. Fine, if he was so sure, I'd give him want he asked for. Soon he'd be fighting for breath.

I bore down with my hips in smaller and smaller circles until he was against my g-spot. He seemed comfortable as I rode him, so I put a hand on the headboard, and the other on the wall, this time for leverage. Zade's third tongue lapped at the edges of my entrance even as I was filled by the first. He couldn't see them, but he managed to find my wrists and pulled them from the wall and the headboard. I sank deeper onto his face and he *still* pulled. He wanted the weight. He wanted to wear me, eat me, devour me.

He pulled on my shoulders, compressed my back. My ass dug into his chin. His second tongue entered me, thrilling me. I made use of the leverage he gave me, losing focus as he thrust against my g-spot. Muscles strained and mind bent as pleasure screamed through my body. Warmth flooded my pussy as I squirted, tightening around his tongues. The third flicked my clit, sending an entirely different frequency ricocheting through me. I bore down and tumbled into another wave of pleasure. Damn, that had never happened before. But, of course, I'd never sat on an alien face before either.

I moved to get off of his face, but he held tight to my arms. Without them, my head was too close to the wall to get up and my legs were caught up behind me. He pushed his tongues into me, and pulling away wasn't enough to gain clearance. I was sensitive. My toes curled and my eyes squinted. I looked down to him in hopes he would take pity. His mouth still on me, I could make out his smirk. The answer was *no*.

"Are you still trying to convince me I'm the perfect size?" I squirmed against the overstimulation.

He nodded and, mercifully, stilled his tongues.

I found a deeper breath. "I got it."

Fuck, the pain of spankings was short, easier to endure than his teasing punishment. His intensity unlocked something in me though. Maybe I was perfect, powerful, strong. He let go of my arms and let me climb off his head. I wasn't allowed far. He wrapped his arms around me and spooned me. "Next time you act like your size is a problem, I will absolutely worship you until you're begging me to stop. You are perfect."

All the need and argument had been wrung from me. Zade was bigger and stronger than any of my other boyfriends. He needed, enjoyed, wanted my body, no matter how pregnant—or maybe especially because of it. We were perfect, and any doubt that I wasn't was going to be swiftly punished.

…though I still found other ways to earn the spike and sting of his spankings.

Chapter Forty-Seven
Honesty and Jewelry

Zade

Cassie lounged with a poetry book resting on her massive belly. I was out of my cast and sitting on the floor next to her so she'd be as comfortable as possible. Perhaps it was mean, but I hoped she stayed pregnant for as long as possible. She was so freaking hot like that, round and swollen.

Spending the weeks in recovery and away from the mines would have been torturous—in fact, I'm sure I would have set up in the office and run things from there had it not been for Cassie. Instead, I stayed home, and I found that with her in my life, I didn't miss the mines. I lived each day to make her laugh. It bounced off the cave walls more brightly than anything else.

I offered to read from my father's journal more, but Cassie was much less interested in holmium as of late. I read it beside her. I learned he reached the same point with his nose and ability in finding glor. He thought it had to do with the balance of minerals in the soil around us when we're born. As we dig deeper, we need to calibrate with a new generation of Xavian glor-finding noses. We could still be reaching the end of a finite supply, but his theory gave me hope for glor's future.

Glor's future was no longer *my* future though. That's where my father and I would diverge. I would focus on the family Cassie and I would create. I'd be a good partner and father, or at least give it as much dedication as I'd previously given glor. My dad taught me to persevere and hold on…and I'd do that with my love and heart, Cassie.

I would be with her, create with her, and love with her. I would love our children, no matter their species, no matter their genetic material. I would be able to love better *with* her. Fuck holmium and fuck glory, I would trade it all for the possibility of growing old with Cassiopeia, my woman from the stars.

This strange mixture of contentment and excitement was something I'd never experienced, and the jewelry in my pocket increased it ten-fold. The jeweler did not take long to do as I requested. The most time-intensive and difficult part was shaping the gemstones. I did that myself when I returned to the mines. This cut into my work, because I refused to spend any extra time away from Cassie, especially when she was close to giving birth.

I told Cassie she could wait and learn to read with her child, but she remained dedicated to learning our written language because she enjoyed our poetry. More than Earth poetry she said. When she requested the translation of a word, it gave me my idea.

"Let me test you," I said. I pointed out some words to her and had her read them out loud, picking through the page so that I could get her to say what I wanted.

"I…made…this…for…you," she said. It took her a few moments to realize that she'd said a sentence. Then, "Wait, what?"

Between my finger and thumb, I had the minute nose ring with jewels from the mine.

"This is for me?" she asked, tears immediately edging her eyes. She cried so easily. "I've never had something so beautiful. You made it?"

"I found the gold and the…" I trailed off, unsure of the right words.

"Emerald and aquamarine, I think," she supplied for me, still staring at the jewels.

"Yes, and I cut and polished the gemstones, and had a jeweler set them for us. I have a matching gold bar and chain to put on," I said.

We adorned each other with jewelry. I didn't know if we'd develop rotha marks like purely Xavian couples, but I didn't think it was coincidence that Cassie and I had the only nose piercings on Xavia. I attributed it to rotha. Across galaxies we'd found each other, and we'd always be able to seek out and find each other. This jewelry symbolized that.

"This is really special. Thank you. I've never had anything crafted for me." Her eyes welled up again and threatened to spill over.

Cassie sat up and had me sit on the urish with her. She gave me a hug. "I've never been treated so kindly." She snuggled close to me, and I couldn't imagine anyone treating her differently. She deserved the best. I would spend the rest of my life caring for her and destroying any worry she had about anyone else. Her father could come with an armada. The Orkain could attack in flocks. No one would hurt her. I would always keep her safe.

It bothered me when no one came to look for us after we were carried off by the Orkain. We couldn't give up like that anymore. Things would need to change here, and I would spearhead it if necessary. I had a new mission with Cassie in my life—to protect her and keep her safe. She was the love of my life.

Chapter Forty-Eight
Burning Heart

Cassie

"When are these rotha pains supposed to fade?" I asked, rubbing my chest, thankful he'd come back home from the mines.

"Possibly not until I impregnate you," he said.

"But I'm already pregnant! Who knows, this could be heartburn from that, not rotha pains at all." Even after months, I still wasn't sure what was pregnancy-induced and what was rotha-induced. Everything was new and strange. I could only roll with it.

"Heartburn?"

I described the sensation of heat rising in your chest and throat and making you want to swallow.

He nodded enthusiastically. "It feels like your heart is burning. That's a good one," he said as if I'd come up with the play on words myself.

Sure. He could think I made that one up.

"No, I don't have pain like that. It's more like a dull thumping."

I nodded but regretted it as my heartburn returned to the surface. I would be happy when I had this baby out of me. I might have been in stasis for part of it, but that did not stop me from feeling like the pregnancy was taking far too long. I felt like a balloon. A gassy, flaming balloon.

But I also felt strangely at home. The cavern was such a sweet place to give birth and raise a family. I couldn't imagine any place safer for little Cash if it was a boy—or I didn't know if I could resist Andromeda as a name for a little girl. She traveled into space, millions of light years, and that was Cassiopeia's daughter.

Either way, we'd have no problem staying here on Xavia, learning and trusting in a new way of life. Was that overconfident of me? Probably. But pregnancy and love and rotha had turned me into someone a little different, someone who desired to have more—even the stars—for her little ones. If my dad came back, he would only be able to admire how I'd built myself a life here too. How it was never me that was the failure. Neither I nor my mom was the common denominator in our struggles. I wasn't letting him control me anymore. I was free.

I found my own purpose. Not just Zade or my future children, but as a pioneer in space, time, and intergalactic relations. I was a part of something huge for not only Xavia, but humans, and for my soul. I finally felt full.

So it was like a sucker punch to the gut when Zade announced the news. "The scouting team found an outpost of twenty Orkain living in caves."

"In caves? But that's where we live." The caves were supposed to be safe. And even though ours was isolated, I didn't like that we were seeking the same homes.

"Vance was on the scouting trip. I hope now he and the prince will realize we cannot move our cities underground."

I agreed, and not just because my rotha mate enjoyed the mines. I didn't want my children to never see the sun. "Are they thinking of attacking?"

"They haven't told me, but I think about how it will be safer if they are gone." Zade had a distant look. Was he thinking about the day I'd been taken?

"Maybe that's the cave I would have been taken to," I wondered out loud. No one went to look for us. Was the woman that had been taken months ago alive in that cave?

If it had been me, I would want someone to still be looking for me. I would want them to attack the Orkain and get me back. Were there other Xavians imprisoned? The Orkain weren't native to this planet. "We need to fight back," I said, surprised by my own conclusion.

I'd always been the hippie rebel against my father's military background. Make love, not war. Maybe I'd changed my mind because I was about to be a mother, or because I realized I could have easily been left to the Orkain. Would I or my baby have survived?

Zade's eyes went from distant to direct. "What if they ask for volunteers in the fight?"

"You want to volunteer? You have a military for that."

The Xavians had many people already dedicated to protection and to fighting the Orkain. Zade was doing his duty already, more than his duty. He was working the mines and keeping up their entire industry as well as now building a family with me to extend the Xavian legacy. Did he also have to fight hand-to-claw?

Zade's jaw tensed. "I keep thinking about if I hadn't run and landed just right on that Orkain, that I could have missed it and you, and you would have been gone."

"…in that cave," I finished.

"In that cave," he repeated.

The thought of Cash or Andromeda stillborn in another, darker cave came unbidden. I understood Zade's desire. Even though I didn't have any military or fighting background, I wanted to rush that cave and punch an Orkain myself.

"That doesn't mean you need to lose your life in there though." At the same time, I wondered how we could continue to live if we learned some of our people were imprisoned.

He kissed the top of my head. "My love, my love," he said. He couldn't deny it was dangerous.

"I trust you." It felt weird to say that. Not just because all the brat and daddy play recently, but because I'd never been in this sort of relationship…the trusting kind. But Zade had changed my perspective on so much. It was a whole new world, literally and personally for me. All of my running away had been running towards him, towards home. I'd found it. "If you think you will be of help and want to go, then you should go."

"You are starting to learn who is the master of the house." He puffed up his chest.

I gave it a playful smack.

His hand circled around my wrist, keeping me from escaping. "Don't hit the master. Do you need a lesson?"

"Uh, only if it won't worsen my heartburn."

"I am a merciful master. You may receive your spankings standing, arms and legs spread."

"Yes, daddy," I said, thankful I wouldn't have to bend over. I would pay my penance, and then I'd think of something else naughty to do.

Obedience and trust were two different things, and I enjoyed playing with Zade. He was a dream.

Chapter Forty-Nine
Before I Go

Zade

Months ago, Vance and Sara experienced rotha bonding too. Both covered in rotha marks, they had a kumirata broadcast on the settit in a big extravagant affair. Cassie and I giggled at the pompous display, but it did symbolize a permanent connecting of our peoples.

Cassie and I didn't need a big ceremony. I'd always been a private person, and Cassie didn't know any of the other women except Layla. Those two talked on the settit most of the day still. However, I noticed the finger rings Vance and Sara exchanged. It was a human tradition they'd included. Remembering how much she loved the nose ring, I had a finger ring made for her too. I had picked it up from the jeweler earlier today.

We sat in bed, and I examined her body and she examined mine for rotha marks. It was our new nightly routine, and it more than usually led to more intimate moments. This night felt a little different though with what hung over us tomorrow. I'd be attacking the Orkain in their home.

"I'm worried," she said.

"I'm not." That's what I was supposed to say, right? "You and I are rotha. Why would you fly all the way here for me to die senselessly?"

"Dude, that's war."

"*Dude*, we are forever," I said, using her own word against her. I pulled the ring from my pocket. "For my love, because I will be back." I traced the circle of the ring to indicate a coming back, a returning.

"This isn't for my nose, is it?" she asked examining it.

"No, your finger... Vance and Sara had finger rings as part of their ceremony."

"Are you asking me to marry you?" Her brows furrowed questioningly, but her smile grew larger and larger.

"If that's your forever, then yes."

"That's my line."

"What?"

She laughed at her own joke and then put the ring on her left hand, like they did in the kumirata. I think I had done all right. "Yes, let's do this forever-thing."

I marveled at how far we'd come. Light years away physically, then enemies, and now my lifetime mate. "What would you like to do tonight?" I asked her.

Cassie leaned forward and kissed me. Her lips tasted so sweet. I loved glancing down at the gold sticking out from her nose. It was a small piece of jewelry, but it suited her. We made out until she began to get restless. Rather than have her roll over, I replaced my body with a few pillows and moved to the other side of the bed to "spoon" her.

While there were times she'd been too uncomfortable to enjoy sex, she had now been asking quite frequently. She thought it would induce labor. I didn't know if that was medically true, but I wasn't going to argue with her. I'd been helping her orgasm multiple times a day, as much as she could stand, because she wanted to have her baby. Tonight wasn't any different.

I ran my hands over her body constantly, up and down, around, across and over. I thought she'd grow tired of it, but it seemed to soothe her. Her skin was so soft. I couldn't get over it or over her.

Cassie enjoyed the touch of all our body parts. Her ass moved rhythmically against my cocks which wetted between her cheeks. I snuggled a hand below her tummy, wrapped in warmth and massaged. I loved the way my fingers slipped over slick flesh. I drew circles around her clit, unhooding it. I made the same circles with fingertips on her nipple. My cocks twitched as her pleasure escaped in sighs and moans. Somewhere, we lost the language barrier and communed in something that was more than English or Xavian. It was purely us.

Her tummy commanded space as she began to breathe heavy. My cocks pressed against the roundness of her butt with each pant from her lips. They wanted in on the action, but this was all about Cassie. It was always about Cassie.

I increased my motion but only just so. She tended to get uncomfortable quickly. I wanted to take this slowly to ensure she could sustain to a finish. I skipped over her clit and got a murmur of disapproval.

"Please? I want to cum," she said quietly as if others could hear.

I didn't even think about giving in. I nibbled on the shell of her ear to distract her from the building need in that pussy. I knew what she needed. When she directed the pace, she'd often work herself up into a frenzy in which her orgasms became difficult and evasive. Instead, I kept up an even level of arousal, edging her close, then pulling her away a few times until there would be no stopping it.

That was the plan anyway, but as I massaged her sore, aching breast, she squirted in my hand. It surprised me and turned me on much more than I anticipated. Liquid dripped between my fingers. My cocks flinched. I quickened my pace against her clit, too excited.

"Yes, Daddy," she muttered, possibly unaware of her leaking breast, only of the effect on me. Fuck, I decided I couldn't go back now; she was trusting me to get her through to orgasm. I licked at her ear, flicking and sucking on the lobe at the same frequency as my fingers on her clit, my hand frozen at her breast.

I felt her muscles contract and her belly extend and shift as she curled into an orgasm. My fingers danced on her clit as she cried out. I didn't let go of the pace until her pitch changed and I knew she'd reached her maximum. Her giant pregnant belly and her desperate plea for relief was such a fucking turn-on.

"Fill me," she pleaded

Mentally, I hesitated, but my cocks didn't wait for me. Even as my hand slipped from below her belly, they slipped between her legs. She and I were both slick.

Her back tensed. I put a guiding hand on her hip and encouraged her to relax. My cocks could contract and extend once inside her with less bumping and bouncing than sexual relations with a human male. And for as pregnant as Cassie was, it was best to only give her one or two dicks and play with that area she called the g-spot.

I slid in one of my dicks. She felt so fucking good, her pussy tight, wet, and pulsing. With the baby in her tummy, she was stuffed, overfull. She moaned in a gray area, possibly between pleasure and struggle. Our hands found each other. I wrapped my fingers around hers supportively as I stroked deep. Then I retreated my length to tease and massage her g-spot with my head.

This shallower sex drove her crazy. She was too big to wiggle around. Instead, she let strings of sexy words escape her. She told me just how good I was making her feel. The ebb and flow of her murmurs echoed the rhythm of her pleasure. I would tease out babbling nonsense as her words and senses gave out.

I massaged her breast and was rewarded with warm milk between my fingers. Her body was sex and creation perfected. I sunk deep into her heat.

"Will you cum with me?" she breathed. The raspy need in her voice and the tightness of her pussy made declining her invitation impossible. I would gladly do as she requested. I picked up the pace.

She cried out my name, and her pussy constricted around me. I pumped, filling her channel with my seed. My other cocks followed, and with each orgasmic release, she praised me, her pussy rhythmically tightening around my sensitive dicks. Fuck, I was going to put a child in her as soon as this one came out.

I loved diving headfirst into this relationship, a baby already on the way. Our family would be perfect. It was meant to be. I knew, because Cassie was my rotha. This was our family. I slipped out and got a warm washcloth to clean my beautiful mate. She thanked me, her voice still honeyed and warm. I cuddled next to her as she began to fade. She'd had trouble sleeping the last few nights because of the baby, so I was extra careful to be quiet and keep her comfortable until I heard her soft snoring. My hand on her belly, I prayed the baby would allow her rest before making its arrival.

Chapter Fifty
Goodbye

Cassie

I wasn't one of those patriotic women who shook a damp hankie as they waved their husbands off to war. Neither was my mom, apparently. So while I didn't say it out loud, I secretly hoped I would go into labor in the morning and that would serve as enough of a distraction to keep Zade here with me instead of heading off with the soldiers.

Unfortunately, I woke up still solidly pregnant. Uncomfortably and annoyingly so. I was pissed, but it was difficult to stay angry when my doting mate was helping me at every chance. Even though he was preparing for the first offensive attack on the Orkain, he was also helping me dress. He fastened a top back button that I worried I wouldn't be able to unfasten myself. I couldn't find my voice to state the worry though as his lips touched my neck. He knelt down, helped me into clean panties, and put warm socks on my swollen feet before they touched the cave ground.

He was so good to me. I wanted to tell him to not go, a million times over. However, our lives had already been put at risk once. Our small family fought for survival, and now we'd fight to have safe lives on Xavia. Zade's expertise on caves and explosives was needed for their attack. He was critical to the mission.

I was proud of him, but I was also fucking scared.

After he dressed me and fed me, he left. The tears washed away his sweet kisses from my skin. I wept for what we might lose. Layla and I called each other soon after. Layla had switched and, after the tiniest stint ever with Prince Drex, was now with Chelk. Chelk was in the military, a warrior, and so was in on the attack too. I hoped there wasn't anything like a phone bill on Xavia, because Layla and I stayed on the line all day. It was like having virtual company over. It was good to have a friend during uncertain times.

"What's Chelk like?" I asked, trying to get my mind off Zade and the bulbous growth that refused to be born.

"He's a grumpy asshole, but there's something kind in there too."

"Are you sure? Cause you led with grumpy asshole." Chelk had already failed with his first human guest, and Layla, who was the sweetest person I'd ever met on Xavia or Earth, was calling him out.

"He endured an apocalypse as a warrior. Of course he has a hard exterior. I won't hold that against him."

Ugh. It reminded me of the military wives enduring abuse and infidelity. "Okay, well remember, you don't have to settle for the asshole. There are other Xavians and they all believe in rotha. They won't hold it against you if you two aren't a match."

Layla nodded. I hoped she was absorbing my advice. I'd escaped so many assholes, and I didn't want

Layla to have flown across the entire galaxy just to get stuck with one here.

It was weird to have gone from feeling so lonely on Earth to having a lifetime mate and a best friend in the handful of people I knew on Xavia. I loved my little world, but I was also excited for it to get bigger with the appearance of whoever popped out.

"Any day now," she said in a way that changed the topic back to me and this never-ending pregnancy. "Have you thought about a name if it's a girl?"

"I have. Andromeda is Cassiopeia's daughter in mythology."

I'd been embarrassed by my name as a kid, but on a different planet, it fit me. A name for the stars.

"I like that—Andromeda for the first human girl born off-planet."

I nodded, my face falling a bit thinking about the future and worrying about Zade.

"How are the rotha pains?"

"Not bad, actually," I said. We'd spent so much time together that the intensity seemed to have faded even though I couldn't yet be pregnant with his child. At the moment, it felt like sharp nails in my side. Pleasant, right?

"Any marks like the sisters?"

I shook my head. Sara and Katy had exhibited actual skin changes like the Xavians. Despite having the same pains they described, I hadn't found any marks. Of course, I could only see so much of my body right now. Maybe I would experience changes postpartum. Maybe I couldn't with someone else's baby inside me.

Even without the marks, I knew for sure that Zade was my rotha mate. I experienced the rotha pain, the burning when he was gone, and the relief when he returned. I hadn't asked Heljin or Zade if I would be able to sense if Zade died. I didn't want confirmation of what I knew in my heart.

I'd absolutely fucking know.

Chapter Fifty-One
Loss

Zade

The rotha pains felt less punitive and more like confirmation that I was doing the right thing by leaving my mate to fight the Orkain. Amongst the warriors, I was easily the thinnest man. Xavians believed strength and muscle would win. Vjann, leader of pointy sticks, was probably about my father's age. He was a stocky man but walked lightly. I'd never been part of the military or joined in any scouting missions. I had never felt the need or been needed. However, they wanted to use explosives to close the cave entrance, and I was the most knowledgeable.

Unfortunately, their inclusion of me seemed to be the extent of their smart decisions. That became abundantly clear when we arrived at the wrong cave. We were farther north in a different rock face than they'd told me. I attempted to approach Drex, but Vance played guard to the prince's attentions.

"This is the wrong cave—" I started.

"No, I've been here. This is the right cave. They are in there," Vance said, cutting me off.

I held my temper. I remembered the phrase Cassie had used, "brains over brawn." To solve problems, I would have to convince others of the solutions. Drawing attention to the fact that Vance had pointed out the wrong cave on a map wasn't going to get me anywhere.

"I'm sorry. I measured the dynamite and subsequent explosion for the wrong cave," I said, taking the blame.

"What does it matter?"

I wasn't getting through to him, which meant I wasn't going to be able to get to Drex. "The density of the rock is different here, and the floor could be much lower. The explosion might not even touch the Orkain's roost. You can't fight gravity." It wasn't all completely true. It wasn't all completely untrue either. I swallowed hard. It was difficult to play political games while trying to avoid horrible, potentially fatal mistakes.

"Are they really that different?" asked Vance, uncertain.

The interaction had taken long enough to garner the attention of Drex. I had my chance. "Sir, this is a different cave than I calculated, I'm sorry," I said, being careful not to blame Vance or Vjann for the clear mistake. "I recommend delaying the attack until we can verify we have enough dynamite power to collapse the chamber."

"We still have surprise on our side. We have everyone here to attack them even if they're merely incapacitated. I'm not sure if we need to stop. We may never get another chance like this if we give away our position now," said Drex thoughtfully, thankfully not deferring to his adviser quite yet.

"We could still have surprise if we pull out now and carefully hide our tracks. If we can rightly collapse the cave, we'd have no casualties on our side," I suggested.

Vance had described tunnels in the ceiling of the cave which I thought led to a different cave system, but this cave was isolated. It wouldn't have made any sense to create tunnels. If they led to a chamber, Xavians or humans wouldn't be able to exit the vertical tunnels without falling into the rocky pit that had stopped the scouts from venturing any farther into the cave previously.

This was the longest I had ever had Drex's ear without Vance butting in. I took my chance. "And if possible, we need to verify where their tunnels lead. There could be exit tunnels. Or they could have created a chamber above them for captives."

"Captives? Our people alive? Fryyre," Drex's voice went distant as he considered the possibility. "We can't risk using explosives if our people are in there."

That's the conclusion I had hoped Drex would reach. He barked an order to Vance who stomped off toward Vjann and his warriors. It felt like a relief to only have to convince one Xavian, and he ordered the others. It had been so difficult to get enough people to understand, and not have their feelings hurt in the process, that I had just about given up on Xavian government. But now I had a bigger reason. I was making the world safer for Cassie and our brood. And that meant figuring out how to speak in a way that got others to listen.

We retreated and hid our tracks as best we could. If the Orkain learned we were here, they could relocate and attack would be impossible. Or they could lie in ambush when we returned. There was risk involved in our decision, but it was the right choice. I was glad I had volunteered to come. I didn't want to think about what could have happened if I'd calculated the explosive and provided it to them without escort. I had a renewed sense of purpose. Even if we stopped needing glor, I was still useful to the Xavians. I couldn't control everything in the mines or out here, but at least today, I felt I had done all right.

We turned back and I went home.

#

Cassie threw her arms around me, "Home so soon?"

I shared with Cassie about the cave, about the possibility of captives. "Without wings, you can't get out. It's a perfect prison. I couldn't let them bomb it." I hung onto her as if she could still be torn from my arms and taken there. I choked over my apology. "I'm sorry I couldn't make this world safer for you tonight."

"But you did," she said, pulling back to look at me. "You kept those possible victims safe. I could have been in there. I'm much safer because you are here. I trust you and I love you."

She loved me. Not because of the protection I promised or because I mined valuable glor, but because of the way I conducted myself. Who I was, not what I could do. And I'd do that without her love, so it was that much more special that she did love me.

"You are amazing. I love you too. Now sit down and let me massage your legs."

"Do my ankles look that bad?" she asked wryly.

They had swollen to the size of her calf. "They look painful," I said and took her feet upon my lap. I was thankful to be here for her. Keeping her well seemed

the most important duty of mine. I would be dedicated
to it.

Chapter Fifty-Two
Daddy

Cassie

After my foot massage, I got up from the couch to pee. By the time I returned, Zade had fallen asleep. From behind, I could see his intact horn moving with each of his snores. The other we were in process of filing and smoothing. He'd lost that saving me, and tonight he was tired from saving who knows who in that cave. Prisoners being kept by the Orkain? It would be a dream come true if some Xavians were alive…but a nightmare for those being kept. Nothing could be done tonight though. Except me.

I'm sorry, but if Zade thought that almost going to war and a foot massage was going to save him from his duty of pounding this baby out of me with his cocks, he was sadly mistaken. Him being back home just made having this baby the next task on my to-do list. While stasis on the ship had mussed up the timeline, I was certain I was close. And while I'm a brat, I'm not *evil*. I let him sleep for a while before throwing a pillow down between his feet and getting down on my knees. If anything, Zade would have to wake to help me return to standing.

I crept my hand over his muscular thigh to the ties on his pants and began loosening them. He judged me from beneath heavy eyelids. "Even tonight?"

"I want to make you a daddy," I said mischievously.

"They cannot call me daddy," he said, frowning.

Understandable. He only knew 'daddy' from my lips. "Papa then. Or, what is it in Xavian?"

"Hah-za."

"Aw, that's nice," I said, tucking that piece of information away for later.

"Are you comfortable?" he asked, concerned. He grabbed a pillow from the couch to provide me more comfort. I put it between my ass and calves, propping me up and putting less strain on my knees

"I want your cock."

"Impatience," he scolded playfully. "I should teach you a lesson."

I rolled my eyes and busied myself with his laces again. He put a hand on my two. Larger, they effectively stopped me from undoing his pants.

I looked up at him coyly. He was no longer sleepy-eyed, and the building bulge underneath my hands revealed I was getting to him. My smile faltered when he punished his impatient brat.

"If it is good-feelings you seek to encourage your body to give birth, you will receive them, but not in a rushed chore. You will receive in dabbles and dribbles, riding on ripples, not waves."

His fingers traced and teased up my arm but at much a slower pace than I'd set up. He let go of my hands but still guarded his crotch.

He might be limiting his touch of me, but I could touch myself. A hand on each breast, I began to massage circles toward the nipples. My boobs were heavy and ready to provide life for my little one. Zade's breath hitched. I had his attention now. I figured I might. I felt a bit of relief as I drew liquid and rubbed it into my skin.

"You are so beautiful full of life," he said, eyes glued to my chest. "And you want this cock to fill you more?" His hand, supposedly protecting his cock, swept over his pant seam in a way that wasn't exactly subtle.

Fill me more wasn't really what I was after. It was more of a "Him in, Baby out" sort of thing. But I wasn't going to voice a correction and slow down the foreplay.

I held my tongue and nodded instead, supporting my weeping breasts with each hand. Ah, I knew how to speed this up. "Do you want your cocks between these breasts?" I asked. "All of me is wet for you."

That did it. Zade's pants were quickly undone and he sat fully erect. I grinned over his cocks, slick with pre-cum, before pressing them against my milky boobs. His ridges rubbed my swollen glands. I thought he'd lose it when I titty-fucked his cocks, dipping my mouth over the heads as they popped out between my cleavage. The stimulation brought forth more milk. Zade didn't cum, but he did forget the idea of long foreplay.

He helped me to my feet, intending to escort me to the bed, but I was much too needy for that process which would undoubtedly include many pillow props and, worse, possibly mood lighting and other atmospheric tweaks. So instead, I leaned over, two hands on the couch back, and invited him to put those milk-soaked cocks into me while standing.

"Fryyre," he mumbled, taking in my body. He roughly sidled against me, leaned over, and whispered in my ear, "Perhaps you can learn your lesson on impatience another day."

My brat girl smile returned, even as he treated me well. He grabbed a sturdy pillow and placed it between my arms so I could rest my upper body if I got tired. Then he slapped my booty so hard it made all my cheeks jiggle before sliding his length between my legs. A doubt and a thrill went through me as I marveled at the size difference; *those massive cocks* somehow fit inside me.

I wanted him to spear me over and over again, knocking on my cervix until that baby decided to drop out of me. I wanted relief from my swollen tits. An arm hooked at my side, providing me extra support as he positioned the head of the biggest cock at my entrance. Christ, that's what I needed. Another hand gently massaged my tits, and milk dribbled down my curves to where Zade and I were connected.

With his own needy groan, he sank his cock into my wanting heat. And I lost focus on wanting to be done, and to be farther along the trail of this pregnancy and birth. He held me so supportively. For the first time in…ever…I felt weightless. I felt one with him. Warm desire grew inside me as he contracted and extended along my channel, no uncomfortable bumping of hips needed.

Even as my pussy began to tighten, he slowed his motion. Bratty me would have pointed that out, but even here, I was on the edge of bliss. My eyes blinked rapidly as I tried to discern and enjoy the minute touches he was giving me. They rolled back when one cock unwrapped to play with my clit in slow gentle waves. I felt pure contentment. My toes curled as I'm sure my knees gave way. Zade was there to hold me and fuck me until even my bloated pregnant ass was a puddle.

When I was done, I rolled over as gracefully as I could, which I admit was a much slower event than I anticipated. Big, round, and on an oversized couch was a lot of physics to overcome. But I settled into his arms, both of us content with how things had turned out.

"That's the way to do feel-good hormones," I think I heard him say.

I was drifting off. That's the way, indeed.

Epilogue
Tell Him

Cassie

"Oh, they're beautiful! We're going to ruin them." I laughed as Zade brought in some absolutely lovely rugs hung over his arm.

They were the colors of Xavian sunrises and the verdant jungles beneath them. I had him bringing in lots of rugs, because Cash was crawling and I was so scared of him scraping his little body on the cold cave floors. Zade first had to convince me not to move us somewhere else entirely so we could have "real floors." We compromised, since this cave was the safest place to raise a family. We'd stay and he would get me absolutely any number of rugs I needed to feel safe as a mom. Ha, he had absolutely no idea what he was getting into. I had them overlapping and stacked. I even made bumpers for the corners. As soon as the kid stood up, I was going to start tacking them to the walls.

But true to his word, Zade brought rugs home every day. And every day he helped me wash rugs that had been mussed. Sure, the cave floor would have been easier to clean without them, but I couldn't help myself. Maybe I would relax more with our second child. There wouldn't be any Xavian tapestry history left if my children vomited on all of it.

But it was difficult to relax with the threat of the Orkain over our heads. After better intelligence and heavy surveillance of the Orkain cave, they'd been no closer to learning if prisoners were being held. The prince decided it was too risky to use explosives and instead had individual Orkain followed and killed. There would be an invasion to follow. Zade was no longer part of the planning, but because of his contribution, he was being consulted a lot more.

Zade kissed me over the rugs, then stacked one in front of the kitchen sink for my tired feet. He was so sweet. He replaced the one I had pulled to be cleaned, even though there wasn't any cave floor to be seen, and that made *me* feel seen. Zade went over to Cash, who was sleeping, of course. How did Zade always luck out like that? I'd spent all day trying to get Cash to nap, and I was hardly ever successful until just before Zade came home to enjoy the silence. One day, the pregnancy hormones got to me, and I asked if he sat outside and waited for the baby to stop crying before he entered. And he looked at me, so surprised that I knew immediately it wasn't the truth. After he soothed my frazzled nerves, he "punished" me with a good spanking.

I trusted and loved my partner, but my mouth got the better of me so often. That's how I shined as a brat. It got me in trouble and my ass spanked frequently. Zade started carrying a handkerchief around. The silky fabric between my teeth and on my lips became an instant turn-on, like Pavlov's stupid dogs, but it wasn't my mouth that watered. Then I'd get that stinging slap from his hand, or from something pervertible within reach. I loved the kitchen spoon so much that I started keeping it in the bedroom until Zade told me it was his grandmother's favorite spoon too. Back into the kitchen it went. He gave me a replacement when I had been particularly good, or bratty. I forget which. It was a gift, but it was a punishment? Whatever. The rules get fuzzy.

"You two are my treasure," he said, getting back from staring at Cash. I lost a lot of time watching him sleep too…watching both of them.

"Is that why you're not in the mines as much? We're your treasure?"

"Indeed," he said, kissing my temple before sidling up to me at the kitchen sink where I was washing an endless number of dishes. "That and my next son will have the glor-minding ability and free me of my responsibilities."

"We don't know if that will be the case," I hedged. I didn't want him to get his hopes up when we couldn't know for sure.

"We didn't know until we became rotha-bound. We have the marks. You will have my son. He will have my nose," Zade said confidently. "And if not—*fuck holmium*."

I could agree with that last part wholeheartedly. "Fuck holmium."

I wasn't worried. I could already tell he loved Cash unconditionally. He would love his own son the same. Zade had learned he couldn't find all the glor, but he could learn to mind it. It was no longer the end of our individual worlds. Our world had just started.

He stood behind me and took over the sponge and the dish. It was faster if one of us washed and the other dried, but the way Zade's cocks shifted behind me told me he wouldn't be letting anything dry. I'd never been an instant-on person, but these pregnancies and this man had me switching on like a light switch. Matching electricity and spark, I needed to have my skin on his, to feel him on me, and to get lost with him. For now, we rocked at the sink to silent music, enjoying the quietness. With another baby on the way, this was as quiet as it was ever going to be, one baby snoozing on rugs with other rugs stacked around him like walls. I was content. It solidified my answer. "I've made my decision."

"You did?" He placed the dish he was rinsing into the other sink. Some things were the same on Xavia as they were on Earth, and double sinks were one of them.

"Tell him I died."

My father was on his way back. He had sent me here to spy on these people, but they had become my people. I wasn't going to do any such thing, and I never wanted to go back to Earth. I wanted to stay here with Zade and Cash and whoever this little one was.

"Tell him I was killed in the attack after the landing with the other woman."

My love turned me around, looking into my eyes. We had talked about all the options, but in the end, it was my decision on how to deal with my father. Zade said he would do whatever necessary. He didn't care how it affected the trade of holmium or our relationship with Earth. He wanted me to feel safe.

He pulled me in tight, sealing his promise. "That's what we'll do then."

If the marks growing on my stomach over our second baby were any indication, I felt safe, strong, and healthy here with Zade as we built a future together. At first inspection, the silvery lines looked like stretch marks, but if so, Zade had complimentary sympathetic stretch marks of the same silver color as his hair. I traced where I knew the lines grew on his abdominals, marveling at his taunt, tight stomach. Touching him felt electric, like our atoms were lining up and syncing. My own stomach fluttered. As if Zade knew, he put his hands on my waist.

I still didn't understand Zade's fascination and love for my stomach. Like most women, I didn't like my belly, but Zade loved it so much that it had me questioning a lifetime of self-hatred and comparison. He thought it was sexy, life-giving, and I caught him watching my belly more than I caught him watching my butt.

"I think you're starting to show," he said, his eyes tilted downward, taking in my tits and jutting belly. "Arch your back for me."

I did it for him, popping my stomach out more. It was difficult to hate my body when he pushed me to look more pregnant and bigger. His teeth caught on his bottom lip. There was a sexy twitch to them which I wanted to kiss. So I did, stealing it from him.

He pulled my shirt off. I wasn't wearing a bra, and my breasts lay over my belly. With the exposure, I lactated a bit, my baby sleeping in the other room. Feeling self-conscious, I wiped it with my hand onto my pants.

"No, you smell so sweet," he said, lowering his nose to my neck and collarbone, taking in the scent on my skin. He pulled me close against his body to show me that he didn't care. I had a passing thought that his shirt would be another thing to wash before he captured my lips with his. The urgency and force of his kiss told me we were going to have to wash *everything* between us afterward. Our height difference was difficult to kiss for long periods of time, so he grabbed my legs and sat me on the counter.

I rested my tired arms on his shoulders and ran my fingers through his soft hair. His hands never stopped moving, massaging my neck, roving over my back, grabbing handfuls of ass that bubbled over the counter. I wrapped my legs around him, my clothed mound rubbing on the bulge in his pants.

"You are such a dirty girl though," he said, his breath hot on my cheek.

His cocks shifted between us, possibly fighting amongst themselves to get the best position against my grinding. I found leverage with my heels on his tight butt cheeks and tilted my pelvis toward him, opening me up and bringing my wetness to the surface. He flicked the tip of his tongue inside my mouth as he thrusted between my legs. He wanted to fuck me. I had no objections except our location, and I put my arms around him as he picked me up and moved me to the bedroom.

It was our bedroom now. I'd taken everything out of the room that was his parents and we had decorated together. Zade had now grown up and moved into the master bedroom. His childhood room was Cash's and soon to be shared with our second child. Zade spoke about expanding the cavern as the children grew up and needed more room. I hesitated about the dust. He placed me on the bed, which was far comfier than it needed to be. Suddenly, my mom-tiredness was all over me. If left alone, I probably would have fallen asleep, but Zade remained more focused and attentive. He grabbed handfuls of my pants and panties and yanked them to my ankles and off. Right, sex.

A comment about my wet panties brought me back. His hands explored my body. He started at my ankles, rubbing my calves, circling my knees. Then he pushed my thighs wider, positioning himself between them. I trembled in such a vulnerable position, my pussy open like a feast under his starry, hungry stare. Lowering to me, he slipped his hands underneath my ass to prop me up. My belly fell toward me but his horns were on my skin. And though we had ground and polished the broken one, the asymmetry is enough to remind me how quick and brave he was to protect and save me. This man was everything to me and taking care of me in every way.

He licked circles around my clit and through my folds, lapping up my juices and making my eyes roll back into my head. The circles drew tighter, and I fought to not tighten my legs around his head. I wanted him to hear every hushed moan and coo. I coaxed him toward my clit, but he held off, slowing his tongues until I was pleading softly for him.

Just as desire and agitation were heading each other off, Zade dove a tongue deeply into my cunt while the other two crashed against my desperately needy clit. *Yes.* My entire lower body tightened as both pleasures collided into a powerful orgasm. It could have easily been too much, my toes curling and my jaw popping. He had edged me into oblivion. Somewhere distant, I knew he lapped at me gently as I melted back into my body, our bed, and my bliss.

I did my best to recover as his tongues played and explored my cunt. The gentle pleasure was easy to enjoy. And when I was ready, he rolled along that perfect spot, elevating me to a place that was both here and not quite. My throat dried with unscreamed orgasms, pillows and blankets strewn as other vibrations took over. Zade took me wonderful places. He made me feel like a queen with the oral service until I was dying for his cocks. Starting to feel lonely with no one to kiss, I tugged on his horn, urging him upward to me, unable to use words after so many silent orgasms. It's that desperate urge that destroyed Juliet and Romeo, a clambering to have, need, and be with your destined mate.

The sensation was not too different from his tongues at first. I felt full and happy. Then he sent a dick coiling around the one inside me. My body became fucking electric, Zade's skin dampened against mine, our skin and fresh rotha marks touching. They were a manifestation of the chemical attraction and cohesion between us, but I didn't need them or the baby inside me to know that our bodies created *something else*. My body and soul were unlocked on another level. And besides that, I don't think I'd be easily pleased by a single human cock again.

He kissed me and brought me back to this reality where three tongues French kissed me while three cocks fucked me. I knew what we both wanted next. It had become more difficult, but I twisted around with him still inside me. "Good girl, good girl," he praised as I wound his cocks tight.

He swelled in my channel. A glut of hot seed cut into me to relieve the pressure we both felt. When he untangled inside me, the junction of his cocks conveniently fought for space right at my g-spot, blinding me. I came. And before the mental barrage of how ugly I felt on all-fours could set in, Zade was at my ear, telling me how gorgeous I was, how he loved my tits, my belly, and how he loved holding them. Before I could see straight enough to form an argument, he had pulled out of me and was praising me again with his tongues.

He licked the sensitive edges of my asshole. When I puckered in anticipation, he only responded with equal pressure. I lost it as his tongues pressed inside my pussy and ass. My body shook and eventually gave in. He rimmed me as I came on his tongues, my butt relaxing. Then he was mounting me again, the head of a cock against my hole to replace the training-wheel of a tongue.

The two larger cocks slid in my slick cunt. The flash of intensity gave way to a satisfying sensation as his third entered my ass.

"Good girl, Cassie. You are doing so good taking my cocks."

His praise made me feel braver and relaxed. I dropped to my elbows. That angle was even better. Deep as I wanted, and no banging, only intense waves of pleasurable pressure. I was in heaven.

When one of his cocks pulled out to slide across my clit, I saw stars. I recall asking him to cum inside my ass and it happening shortly afterward. I lost moments, or gained moments. I wasn't sure as my pussy clenched, milking cum from one cock as the other filled my ass.

When the room stopped spinning, I came back to this space and time. This *wonderful* space and time where I shared a cave with Zade who was recovering from his own orgasms. He gently pulled out from me and collapsed beside me, grabbing all that he could of my limbs and curves and bringing them into a delightfully gross snuggle.

"I love you, Cassie. You are amazing."

"No, you're amazing. I needed that. I'll probably need it again in a few hours."

"If you say please," he said sleepily.

I wasn't sure, but we may have drifted off for possibly a few moments before Cash cried for us.

"I'll go get him," Zade said.

He must have needed changing, because he was gone for a while. I almost got up, but then there he was, delivering Cash to me, clean and hungry. As my baby latched on, Zade brought in warm rags for me and cleaned me. I loved the way he treated us, cared for us.

I thought I'd lost the ability to trust people completely. I'd been hurt so much. But love can heal. And when I found someone trustworthy, our love bloomed and healed me. And with Cash, I found I was capable of an even greater love. And what a place for us to thrive, on Xavia with the person we were meant to have in our lives? Zade was my family, my love. My life.

***

Deleted NSFW Scene

Join Reverie's Revelries and get the spicy bonus
scene, *Our Last Night,* as a special gift

Reverieharwood.com/newsletter-spy

A Note for You, the Reader

Dearest Reader,

I hope *My Alien Spy* has added romance, steaminess…and, a little escape…to your day. If you liked it, please review it where you like to buy books. Thank you for your support.

Join me on Ream to read Rotha Mates of Xavia drafts before they're published or to get limited book boxes at https://reamstories.com/reverieharwood. For announcements, my newsletter is good to join. And if you just want to say hi? Write to me at reverie@reverieharwood.com. Talk to you soon.

Here's to more romance in the universe,
Reverie Harwood
September 2024